The Van

I woke up to find my mom pacing in the front room of our house. It was a small house, so it wasn't very hard to notice someone doing anything out of the normal routine. She was lifting the blinds to peek through at the outside. She would spend a few seconds on one side; then shift and spend a few seconds on the other. Back and forth she went. She was peering through as if she didn't want anyone to know she was looking. I couldn't figure out why she just didn't open the blinds all the way and just look at the window. My Dad came up from behind me on his way to work.

"I love her, but you have to admit, she's a bit nuts."

"What is she looking at?"

"There's a van parked at the house where the Cody's used to live."

The Cody family moved away a few months before. My parents liked the Codys a lot. They got along great. Mr. Cody was in the Army, so they moved around a lot. My Mom and Mrs. Cody were friends, but they were not as close as my Mom wanted them to be. She said Mrs. Cody never really got very close to anyone because their family had to move so much it just meant she would be sad about losing touch. The house where they lived had been vacant for while after they moved.

"Who's van?"

"I don't know, but your Mom is on the case."

My Dad gave my Mom a kiss goodbye and went outside. He was just about to get into his car when he turned around and came back to the house. He stuck his head in the front door.

"Carol, I think the plates on the van say California."

He winked at me knowing this would only intensify my Mom's interest and the 'investigation' into our new neighbors.

"California! Boy, that is a long way from here. A long, long way."

Back and forth she went a little bit faster than before. It was a bit weird - I went to bed the night before – no van. The next morning – a van from California parked at the Cody's old house. Weird, but not quite weird enough to hold the attention of a seventh-grade boy. It would take more than that to hold my interest. Back then I was all about surviving the school day, so I could get home and play outside with my friends. An empty van parked in front of an empty house wasn't enough to shift my focus.

The Flush

We were counting down the days until school ended. I think our teachers were too. I usually started counting down the days in September, but by May the countdown would officially start. We were into June, so concentrating was impossible. I thought about baseball most of the time, and girls the rest. I don't remember caring much about girls before that year. It was like someone flipped a switch. I knew next to nothing about what I was feeling. I just knew I started caring about how I looked and how they looked. I liked it when I was close to them and how they smelled. I don't think any of them knew I existed. That was kind of a theme then. I was average at just about everything. Well, I was below average at most stuff if I am being honest. The more years that go by, the closer to average I get.

The eternal struggle for coolness was the overriding effort of my existence in those days. It was tough. There were limited means of raising your coolness in the minds of middle schoolers. I wasn't much of an athlete, and that was how most boys achieved coolness. Getting into trouble was a fast-lane to coolness. That fast lane was closed for me since my parents would have seen to it that all of my new-found coolness was spent within the confines of my room. You could rise to a certain limited level of coolness on the merit of an older brother or sister who had a high degree of coolness. My friend Tommy Howe was cool that way. His older brother, Kenny, was a sports icon in our town, so Tommy kinda rode on his brother's coolness. I was the only child in my family.

Coolness could come through relatives, like it did for Philip Hames. Philip was cousins with the drummer from the Rolling Stones. He had all kinds of Rolling Stones patches on his denim jacket, and he would always be invited backstage when the Stones were on tour. His Mom never let him go though. She said he was too young to attend a rock-n-roll concert. Philip had tons of pictures of the group in his house. He had none though with him and the group together or just him and his cousin. The Rolling Stones drummer never set foot in our little town. The Rolling Stones are from England, and Philip had never set foot outside of New Jersey. Now that I think back, we can probably add lying about being related to cool people to the list of ways in which coolness could be achieved. Well played, Mr. Hames.

Coolness could be reached by playing a cool musical instrument like the guitar or the drums. Some instruments would cost you coolness rather than enhance your standing. Playing the piano or violin had a negative impact on coolness. My mom looked into piano lessons, but we couldn't afford it. It was the first time I can remember being thankful that we couldn't afford something. Now I wish that I could play the piano.

Patty Coyle was cool. She was cool because she was the hottest girl at school. Being hot made you cool too. I couldn't score in this category either. Patty was it. She was the coolest. She was smart, and she was the captain of the softball team. She was the total package. At least as "total" as a seventh grader could be. All the guys at school were into Patty. None more than Todd Hearns. Todd had it bad for Patty. He was always talking about her. Other guys would tell him to shut up all the time – it got old listening to him ramble on and on. Patty had no interest in him at all. It drove Todd nuts.

Todd was always cooking up some stupid excuse to get close to Patty. He would try to meet her as she got off the bus and offer to carry her books or explain that it was important that he take her the homework when she missed school because their families were *really* close. The truth is that the Coyles and the Hearns families hardly knew each other. Our teachers would almost always crush his plans before they got off the ground. Most of Todd's schemes were low risk and low reward. That was the best thing for Todd. His parents were easily the strictest of all our parents, especially his dad. Todd had it hard. He needed to be home the earliest of all my friends, and if he was even a minute late, he'd get grounded for a week. That's why I tried to talk him out of his most elaborate plan ever. We all did. It was dumb. He was sure to get caught, and it just wasn't worth what his Dad would do to him. Todd had it in his head that he was going to find a way to watch Patty get changed for softball practice. He was going to ask for the hall pass just a few minutes before the end of the day. He would sneak downstairs into the girl's locker room and hide in one of the bathroom stalls. Then he would be able to see Patty change through the tiny gap between the stall doors. Dumb. It wouldn't work, and he was going to get caught we told him. In the *very* remote case that it did somehow work, we wanted a full description of how she looked. Todd agreed.

Todd got the hall pass that day just like he wanted. He scooted downstairs somehow undetected and managed to sneak into the girl's looker room. He surveyed the stalls and determined which would give him the best vantage point to see Patty as she got ready for practice. He got inside the stall and waited. The bell rang promptly at 2:45. A few minutes later Todd could hear the low murmur of female voices approaching the locker room. He locked the door to the stall, and he got up in a crouching position on the toilet seat, so no one could see his feet dangling under the stall door. The first few girls filed into the locker room and into Todd's view. They threw their book bags down and opened up lockers across from where Todd was strategically perched behind the relative safety of a locked stall door. More girls arrived and started changing. Some were in full view of where Todd was hiding. Todd couldn't care less about the other girls. He was only there for Patty. Each of the girls started swapping their school uniform for a softball uniform. We were the Angels. The softball uniforms had a huge angel on the front with a bright golden halo over its head. None of girls had a clue about the little devil crouching on a toilet seat just a few feet from them.

Todd's view was even better than he imagined. The gap he was spying though was giving him a great look at almost everything happening just outside his door. Everything, that is, Patty Coyle. She was just slightly out of view, and between her and Todd stood Claire Jablonski. Claire was a nice girl, but she was super heavy when we were in grammar school. The kids would call her 'Jablobski'. Kids can be mean, but don't sweat it too much. Claire grew up to be a fashion model and never gave any of the kids at my school the time of day. You gotta love Karma.

Todd was beside himself. The plan was coming together perfectly, but he just couldn't get a look at his dream girl. He started to shift atop the toilet. He moved desperately from side to side and up and down, but nothing worked. Claire and the stall door blocked everything he cared about seeing. Patty was all but into her softball jersey and Todd was losing it. He thought maybe he could try to peek over the top of the door and over Claire's head. He started to come up out of his crouch when he lost his balance. His left foot sunk into the toilet, and he fell back causing the toilet to flush with a loud old Catholic grade school sound that anyone who ever walked in the hallowed halls of a Saint *Anything* in any town knows all too well. The water gathered toward the top of the bowl now clogged with Todd's left sneaker and overflowed out into the stall and under the door into the locker room. The water just kept running. Some of the girls let out a squeal as the water moved toward them.

The noise caught the ear of Mrs. Hamm. Mrs. Hamm was the girls' softball coach. Mrs. Hamm was in the hallway well into her usual diatribe about how the removal of a school uniform and the donning of the average softball uniform is a process that should take no more than five minutes, but "here at this school for some reason takes closer to thirty minutes", when she stopped mid-syllable to see what exactly was the issue was causing "all this hysteria". Mrs. Hamm hated 'hysteria'. She told all her students about it every day. Mrs. Hamm walked in to see the few remaining "uniform challenged" girls huddling together away from the water flowing into the middle of the room. The next part of the story was disputed by Todd Hearns, but I believe we can assume it to be true based on the number of people who corroborated the detail: Mrs. Hamm heard the sound of sobbing from behind the locked stall door, and she moved to it and knocked loudly.

"Is someone in there?"

"Yes", said Todd. The remaining girls all quickly left the locker room after hearing a male voice from behind the locked door. All, that is, except for Jane Wilton. Jane was clearly born for a leadership role within the Parent Teacher Association of some lucky school in some lucky town. She was definitely a take-charge type who forcefully grabbed the reigns even when there didn't appear to be anything that needed taking charge of. She was unofficially voted most likely to help a teacher write up another student, and she was typically self-appointed to be part of any crisis team that would be charged with getting to the bottom of some situation. Jane's mom was the head of the Parent Teacher Organization for eight year's straight, which was odd because we were only in school for seven at that point. Jane's Mom felt it would take a year of her leadership before Jane started school to get things moving in the right direction. Jane's Mom was unofficially voted most likely to demand a meeting with Principal Hughes.

Mrs. Hamm pulled hard at the door, but it remained locked.

"Open this door right now!"

"I can't", sobbed Todd as has been corroborated by all the witnesses to the event. "I'm stuck."

'What do you mean, you're stuck?"

"My foot is stuck in the toilet."

Mrs. Hamm turned to Jane and told her to go get Mr. Wilbur. Mr. Wilbur was the custodian at the school. Mr. Wilbur was a stickler for organization. He was very detail oriented, but he wasn't very handy. He replaced Mr. Holmes. Mr. Holmes could fix anything, but he wasn't very detail oriented. Mr. Holmes had been 'placed on a new path by God'. Nobody got fired from a Catholic school, not back then at least. I hope the new path involved more sleep because Mr. Holmes was caught sleeping while on the custodian path more times than anyone could count. It earned him the nickname "Sleepy". Mr. Wilbur was definitely much more detailed. Much. More. Detailed. His overalls were pressed, and his tee shirts were always clean and bright. He ushered in the change in terminology at our school from 'janitor' to 'custodian'. He removed the janitor sign on his door and replaced it with a new one that said in large letters 'Custodian'. Just below it he placed another sign that said 'Private'. A third sign said 'Danger'. The fourth sign said, 'Please knock'. The fifth and final sign said, 'God Bless You'.

Jane knocked on the door...as directed. "Who's there?"

"It's Jane Wilton from 7B. Mrs. Hamm asked me to come and get you. There's a boy locked in a stall in the girl's locker room."

Jane smelled something odd. It smelled a bit like burned fish. Mr. Wilbur had his back to Jane and was ironing a pair of overalls while an unknown substance burned on a hotplate nearby.

"There's a what locked in a what? Okay, please step inside but *DO NOT* step past the white line."

Mr. Wilbur looked quizzically at the iron for a means of turning the device off. Failing at that, he pulled the plug out the socket and set the complex machine down. He moved to the hotplate and again appeared to seek out a means of deactivating the machine. After a few seconds he pulled the plug out of the wall and set the pot containing the smoking substance aside.

Once inside the room, one could clearly see the multiple signs that endeavored to express the extreme importance of remaining behind the white line and the mortal danger that could befall someone who was so careless as to move beyond the safe zone. Beyond the white line, the inner sanctum of Mr. Wilbur's office was an ode to school custodial arts. There were more keys than Jane could have imagined existed and certainly more than there were locks in the building. The keys were hanging from a series of color-coded hooks carefully placed to provide wind-chime-like music anytime a gentle breeze moved through from the window in the rear of the room. There were outdoor tools arranged in size order clamped tightly into wall clamps and "enhanced" with custom grips. Mr. Wilbur was big on enhancements. He would provide an unrequested list to Mr. Hughes each Monday of the weekly enhancements he planned on providing. He developed and saved each of the weekly lists on a different floppy disk that he kept locked in his desk. Mr. Stack, the technology teacher, would often suggest saving the weekly enhancement lists to a folder on the school network. Mr. Wilbur said he liked to feel the comfort of having his work in his hands, rather than "somewhere in the air" where any kid with access to a school computer could break his password and delete all his files. This occurred several times before, said Mr. Wilbur, and he was "pretty sure who did it". The culprit deleted all the enhancement files and the only thing left in Mr. Wilbur's network folder was a list of recipes for healthy lunches that could be prepared with a hotplate. On a *completely* unrelated note, the students in classroom 8A would often complain of the odor of burned fish in their classroom, which happened to be directly above the custodial office.

The crown jewel of the custodial enclave was the pegboard. The pegboard was adorned with a myriad of tools that any craftsman would envy. They often came to the school via special delivery and would appear on a second unrequested list provided to Mr. Hughes of "required tooling". The list would detail the tool name, vendor, intended usage, and the purchase price, along with the purchase price of several more expensive sources. Mr. Wilbur was very big on "keeping costs down" and he was often heard reminding students that "just because there was a Sunday collection at mass, it didn't mean that we can all have anything we want". There was a section of the pegboard dedicated to automotive tools, which was odd since the parish didn't own any vehicles at the time.

"Now tell me again what the issue is, young lady."

"There is a boy stuck in a toilet in the girl's locker room. The toilet is overflowing. You need tools to get the door off the hinges and a mop and bucket to deal with all the water in the locker room. I would probably bring some gloves too."

"Whoa now, little lady. I can determine what the right tools are for the job. I don't think someone your age is quite knowledgeable enough to figure all that out on the fly."

Mr. Wilbur pushed a wheeled trash can into the center of the room. He made the item by drilling holes and screwing in wheels on the bottom of a normal trash can. He was very proud of the contraption seeing as how "not just anyone has the ingenuity to put wheels on something, so it's easy to move around". Into the divinely inspired creation he placed several tools to get the door off the hinges, and a mop and bucket to deal with all the water in the locker room. He grabbed a pair of rubber gloves and stored them in his back pocket.

"Lead the way, my fair lady".

Jane rolled her eyes and started toward the locker room.

When Mrs. Hamm was annoyed, she had a habit of pinching the bridge of her nose with her thumb and forefinger while shaking her head. When Mr. Wilbur and Jane got back to the locker room, Mrs. Hamm was pinching the bridge of her nose with her thumb and forefinger, and she was shaking her head.

"Why did that take so long? Why does everything that should take five minutes take thirty minutes here at this school."

"Easy does it. Easy does it, Mrs. Hamm. When young Jane here came to get me, I was in the middle of several things, and I needed to complete them before I could come running down here."

"Can you get the door open?"

"Now what do we have here?"

Mr. Wilbur peered into the gap between the stalls, as he slowly inserted his left hand into a rubber glove. He could see an *allegedly* sobbing Todd with one foot in the toilet and water all around. He stepped back and ran his gloved hand over the door hinge slowly. Anytime there was something to do, Mr. Wilbur would run a gloved hand over the area and say "Sleepy, Sleepy, Sleepy" in reference to Mr. Holmes as though the issue was related to something Mr. Holmes did or failed to do.

"Sleepy, Sleepy, Sleepy".

Mrs. Hamm again had the bridge of her nose tightly pinched. Jane grabbed the mop and walked into the stall next to Todd. She stood on the toilet and reached the mop handle toward the door to the stall where Todd was stuck. She pushed the lock open with the mop handle and jumped down. She placed the mop back in the wheeled bucket, grabbed her hat and glove from a locker, and left. As she walked out, Mr. Hughes walked in. Mr. Hughes was a kind man. As the principal, he had to be tough, but we could tell he hated doing it, and didn't do it particularly well. He had a big belly and his shirt was always wrinkled. His tie rarely made it to third period before twisting slightly and loosening from his neck, so that it hung off to one side. By fifth period he typically had a distressed look on his face as if someone told him something confusing. He could often be heard saying "What the..?" Even at that young age we knew what usually came after 'what the', and we knew why Mr. Hughes censored himself each time he said it. Mr. Hughes moved quickly into the locker room, and instantly into about an inch of a of water.

"What the...?"

"Looks like we have a peeping Tom situation, Mr. Hughes."

Mr. Hughes waded carefully toward the open stall where Mrs. Hamm and Mr. Wilbur were standing. He was clearly reluctant to look inside. He slowly peered around the edge of the stall and caught a look at the boy inside. His head dropped and he let out a huge sigh.

"What were you thinking, Todd?"

"I'm sorry. I'm sorry. You don't have to call my Dad, do you?".

"C'mon out of there."

"I can't. I'm stuck."

Mr. Hughes and Mr. Wilbur walked into the stall. Mr. Hughes held Todd's arm for balance while Mr. Wilbur tried to maneuver Todd's leg out of the toilet. It didn't work. The men tried a dozen different angles and pulled on Todd's arms and legs in multiple ways, but they couldn't get his foot out of the toilet without Todd whining about the pain. Todd apologized to Mr. Hughes about a thousand times, and he asked if Mr. Hughes was going to call his dad about five thousand times. Mr. Hughes just sighed and shook his head. After about ten minutes of trying different things, the men gave up, and Mr. Hughes told Mr. Wilbur to break the toilet apart with a small hand mallet.

Mr. Wilbur chuckled a bit and said "well, I'm not sure a small hand mallet is best tool for that, Sir. I'll go down to the custodial office and bring back the best instrument for this."

When the room was empty except for Todd and Mr. Hughes, Todd really began pleading with Mr. Hughes not to call his dad. Todd was still leaning on Mr. Hughes, but the support was more emotional than physical now. Todd feared his dad immensely. We all did. The only person as upset about the whole situation was Mr. Hughes. There was no way to avoid letting Todd's parents know what happened. It was a call Mr. Hughes was dreading ever since he peaked around the corner of the bathroom stall and saw Todd with his foot in the toilet. It would have been better if it were any other student in that stall, he thought. He was upset because of the fear he felt in Todd's voice and embrace and because he hated what he needed to do. He hated this part of the job above the numerous other tasks he hated doing. He missed being in the classroom, but the pay wasn't good. He wished he could have remained in the math department. He loved teaching and he hated administrating. He decided to go after the principal's job because of money. The money was better, but he hated that money forced him out the classroom. He resented the job for making him unhappy, and he wished he could go back. He knew he was a much better teacher than principal. He walked in hopeful each day and left most days frustrated with himself. He was frustrated now with having to deal with Todd and worse yet, Todd's dad. He hated that Todd put him in this situation. The whole thing came to head after listening to Todd crying and begging for what seemed like forever.

"God damn it, Todd. What choice do you think I have? Huh? Do you think I can just let this go – you sneaking into the girl's locker room to see them undressing? Do you think that it would be ok with Mrs. Hamm if we just swept this one under the rug? Can you just run home and grab some money out of your fucking piggy bank for a new toilet, and we can call it even? Do you think I want to tell your Dad about this? Do you think that's fun for me? Do ya? Do you think I want to be in this toilet with you ankle deep in toilet water instead of driving home right now? Huh? What the hell were you thinking, Todd?

Todd stopped crying and begging and just <u>starred</u> at Mr. Hughes for a second. He was speechless for a minute.

"You said the f-word, Mr. Hughes."

Extra Help

Mr. Woods was my favorite teacher. He was the best teacher I ever had. I had Mr. Woods for Math in fifth grade and never before nor since had I had such an easy time understanding it. He somehow made everything make sense. It was easy when he taught it. He was the teacher we all prayed to have. Most moms started a summer-long campaign to have their child in Mr. Woods math class sometime around the last day of school. The effort continued throughout the summer and intensified as Labor Day approached. My mom refused to call Mr. Hughes to request teachers for the following school year. She would say "you can be successful with any teacher if you work hard enough." I ended up with Mrs. Biggs for seventh grade math. I'm not certain what it was that led Mrs. Biggs to a career in education. I think it was a combination of a deep-seeded hatred of children and a need to inspire frustration in anyone with whom she came into contact. I went to Mr. Woods routinely after school to try make sense of things. It wasn't just math. I would ask Mr. Woods about every subject. I asked him about anything I was confused about. Often it went beyond schoolwork. I learned about life from Mr. Woods.

I was standing in the hallway outside Mr. Woods' class when Mr. Wilbur walked by holding a printout with pictures of toilets and prices in his hand. He stopped and asked me if I saw a red-floppy disk in my travels. I told him that I had not. He went into Mr. Hughes office. I was waiting for Mr. Woods to finish with another student. Mr. and Mrs. Hearns burst out of the front office. Mr. Hearns had Todd by the back of his shirt. Todd was crying and saying 'I'm sorry' over and over. His feet were only touching the ground every few steps because his dad was lifting him up by the shirt collar. Todd's mom was rushing alongside Todd's dad whispering to him to take it easy. I was trying to press against the lockers that lined the hallway to give them enough room to get by. I can remember the look on Todd's dad's face. Mr. Hearns was a big man and he was very intimidating. He glanced at me as they got close. I wanted to crawl into the lockers behind me. Word traveled fast about Todd getting caught in the girl's locker room. All the girls on the softball team knew as did the boy's baseball team and anyone who was still around for an after-school activity. It was a big laugh for everyone, but I wasn't laughing now. I was worried about Todd. Mr. Hughes had come out into the hallway and was watching the family leave the building. Mr. Wilbur stood beside him. Mr. Woods walked out into the hall along with the student with whom he was working. He caught sight of Todd's family at the other end of the hall. Everyone was fixated on the three figures moving toward the end of the hall. I could see the concern on Mr. Woods' face. As Todd and his parents disappeared into the parking lot, Mr. Hughes turned dejectedly. As he started back into his office, he looked up at Mr. Woods. He just shook his head slowly and shrugged his shoulders. Mr. Woods still had the concerned look on his face when he turned and saw me trying to melt into the lockers behind me. He didn't force a smile like most adults do when a kid hears or sees something that they wish the kid hadn't. I'm sure he could see the petrified look on my face. He was just as concerned, but he didn't try to hide it like the rest. I peeled myself off the lockers and walked into his room.

"Did you know Todd was going to do something so stupid?"

"He told some of us. We told him not to do it. We told him it was stupid and he'd get caught."

"Sometimes people can be dead set on running right off a cliff. You can't always stop them. You just need to be there when the hit the ground. Sometimes that's all they'll let you do."

We opened my math book and focused on unscrambling the math that I hadn't learned that day in Mrs. Biggs' class. We never spoke about Todd's locker room episode again.

The Cake

When I got home from school, my Mom was set up in the front room. I could tell how long she'd been there by how many empty Tab cola cans were on the table by the door. There was a weird smell in the house. It wasn't a bad smell. It was actually a very nice smell. It was just not one that I had ever smelled in our house before.

"What's that smell?"

"You see...I'm not the only one who didn't recognize the smell of a cake baking", my Dad said.

"A cake! You're making a cake, Mom?"

"Ok. Let's not pretend that I never bake. I bake. I bake pretty regularly. You people just don't appreciate all that I do around here."

"What kind of cake, Mom?"

I moved quickly to the oven to open it and get a look at the rarity inside.

"Easy. Slow down. It's not ready yet, and I don't want anyone opening the oven just yet. You can look through the glass." It's a...cake cake. You know standard....cake. Yellow cake."

"Mom, never bake cakes", I whispered to my Dad.

"I know. Shhhh."

"Can I put the frosting on it?"

"Frosting. God damn it."

"What's wrong?"

"I need to run to the grocery store. DO NOT OPEN THAT OVEN WHILE I'M OUT."

"So strange for someone who bakes so often to forget the frosting", my Dad said.

"You forgot frosting, Mom? Can we have chocolate?"

"No, I did not forget frosting...I..I need more Tab."

"Shut it, smart ass." My Mom gave my Dad a punch in the shoulder on the way out the door. "And it's not for us".

"What? Who's it for?"

"Our new neighbors." Just calm down. I'll pick you up Twinkies while I'm at the store."

"Our new neighbors???. C'mon!"

"Twinkies are good."

"We never have cake. Why do we have to give a cake to the neighbors? What new neighbors?"

I looked to my dad for emotional support and backup. My Dad just shrugged.

"How was school? Did Mr. Woods help you with the Math?"

"School stinks. Yeah, I get it now. By the way, Todd is going to die tonight. He got caught in the girl's locker room trying to watch them get undressed."

"Wait...what?"

"Yeah, his parents had to come to school and talk to Mr. Hughes. His Dad looked really mad."

"You weren't involved, were you?"

"No. I saw them come out of the front office while I was waiting for Mr. Woods."

"Todd's dad was at school?"

"Yeah. His mom too. They were coming out of office when I saw them."

My Dad struggled to hide one of those concerned faces...just like Mr. Woods did earlier that afternoon. My Dad knew Todd's parents. They would sit together at little league games and sometimes we would see each other at bar-b-ques and birthday parties. My Dad stopped Todd's dad from going on the baseball field once after an umpire made a bad call. He also stopped Mr. Hearns from fighting with one of our other neighbors at a party at The Cody's house. The dads were all playing horseshoes and Mr. Hearns got really mad at one of the other men. I just remember at lot of yelling and then Todd leaving really fast with his mom and dad.

"I got the...diet soda."

"I never knew you could frost a cake with diet soda."

"Jackass."

"Are you really going to give the cake to some neighbors we never met?"

"Yes, it's a nice gesture when people are new to the neighborhood to introduce yourself and give them a cake...or something."

"Can you fit a hidden camera in that cake."

"Knock it off, Smart Ass. I'm trying to be neighborly. I GOT TWINKIES".

"I'm right here, Mom."

"Oh, Twinkies...cool, right? Here, ever had a Twinkie with chocolate frosting on it?"

"Ever had a 12-year-old up all night on a sugar high?"

"Stop it. He's a good kid and he works hard at school. He deserves a treat. Did you hear about Todd Hearns?"

"Yeah, I just heard while you were getting Tab flavored cake frosting."

"Shhh!! Yeah, well our kid isn't trying to watch girls get undressed in the locker room, so be happy."

"I am. I'm just a little worried about Todd with his Dad having to go to school today."

"They called Jim Hearns? Oh boy. I can only imagine what's going on in that house right now."

"Awesome!!"

I wasn't sure I had ever had anything better than a Twinkie with cake frosting on it. Of course, it seemed anything that good always came with a catch.

"So, I'm ~~am~~ going to frost this beautiful cake and then you and I are going to go over there and introduce ourselves to our new neighbors."

There it was.

"Ohhh, no. *Mom…*"

"Hey, it's a nice thing to do when new people move to your neighborhood. Maybe there's a boy your age that lives there. You could be friends."

Any chance of that would be lost once the new kid saw the cake-bearing dork at his front door.

"Why do I have to go? Can you and Dad do it?"

Somehow my Mom did something impossible – she ruined the taste of a chocolate frosted Twinkie. I looked at my dad for support, but he had that look he would get on his face when he knew he needed to back up my mom even though he didn't really want to. It always made it worse when I knew one of my parents were on my side but would just go along for the ride with the other one. I was too upset though. The shame of standing at the front door with a cake in my hands when some new kid who would inevitably be cooler than me and better than me at everything came to the door was too much to bear. There was no way I was going over to the house with my Mom. I might have had a shot at getting out of the embarrassing cake delivery if I had just stuck to begging for mercy. I went with another tactic.

"This is bullshit!"

My mom stopped frosting the cake. Her mouth dropped wide open. I think that was the first time my parents had heard me curse. She turned and started walking toward me with the butter knife still loaded with frosting. I was pretty sure she planned to cut my tongue out with it. My Dad, who had now lost any sense of indecisiveness in the matter, stepped in and took the butter knife from my Mom had before she killed me, or any frosting dripped on the floor.

"What did you just say, young man??"

"Nothing. Nothing, I'm sorry, Mom!"

"Get your little butt in that room and out of my sight until I come for you to bring this cake to the neighbors."

I didn't need to hear that twice. I just about sprinted to my room. I got off pretty easy on that one. Once in my room my attention turned from my good fortune to the intense shame of the upcoming cake delivery. This could not possibly suck any worse. This was going to be the single worst moment in a life full of humiliating and terrible moments to that point. I can remember running through the ordeal in my head as I sat there waiting for my mom. It would be a perfect storm of pre-teen horrors. Our mailman would be dropping off the mail and a milkman would be dropping of some milk as we walked out of the house, although home delivery of milk had ended years ago. The two would laugh uncontrollably at me as would all of our neighbors who would be gathered in front of their homes for some inexplicable reason. Every kid at my school would be in the middle of my street playing in an epic kickball tournament.

The game would stop as the referees, yeah - there would be referees for a neighborhood kickball game, blew their whistles to call a timeout so everyone could watch. I would set a Guinness world record for the number of times getting hit with red kickballs in a sixty-second period. My rich Uncle Bill and Aunt Tina would drive up as we walked toward the old Cody house. My cousin Mark, who my parents called 'the golden child' when they thought I couldn't hear their conversation - who had never received anything less than a 98 on any school-related work, and who was clearly headed for multiple sports scholarship offers and a career in at least two professional sports leagues would get out of the back seat of their luxury car, as twenty-dollar bills blew out of the car door and into the street, and he would hit me in the back of the head with a perfectly thrown football. A bus full of high school kids would surely be stopped in front of the old Cody house. They would be yelling insults and throwing things at me as they took breaks to high five each other. The old Cody house would be filled with cool kids who just moved in and all their super cool friends, and they would all come outside to see just who it was that was delivering a cake to them. My dad would run over when he saw the newest dad on the street holding a guitar. He would act all nerdy and talk about how he's always wanted to learn the guitar but never did. He'd be wearing his sandals with saggy white tube socks. My Mom would explain that the cake was all my idea, and she really didn't have time to bake today, but decided to 'throw something together at the last minute' before gathering everyone around to hear the story about how they nearly went broke when I was little because my prolific bedwetting issues forced my parents to buy a new mattress every month. The festivities would run through the evening all the while I would be holding a plate with a chocolate frosted cake on it. It was all too much to take. My mom finally entered the room to end my mental hysteria.

"Are you crying? Are you really crying about this? This is not a big deal. This is a nice thing that these new people are going to really appreciate."

I wiped away a few tears from my eyes and dejectedly walked toward the front door. My mom held the cake, which was a monumental relief. Neither the mailman, the milkman, nor any of the neighbors were outside. There were no kids, referees, school buses, or kickballs anywhere to be seen. It was just me and my mom and a cake.

"You take it up the door."

"*Mom.*"

"Just do it. It will be nice coming from you. What if they have a boy your age? You could make a new friend. Now hold it straight."

My mom jammed the plate into my unwilling hands and gave me a light shove toward the door. I walked up the few steps and knocked lightly on the door.

"They're not home', I pronounced after waiting an entire three seconds.

"Just wait a minute."

We waited a little while and I knocked a second time. Nobody came to the door.

"Ok, I guess they're out."

I quickly turned and walked down the stairs. That's when I heard the sound of a lock turning and a door starting to open. What a kick in the gut. My best-case scenario was just seconds away and now it was gone. I could have been home eating that cake instead of delivering it. I didn't want to turn around.

"Hello", my mom said. I still had my back to the house.

"Hi."

Wait, that was a girl's voice. I swung around nearly launching the cake into the front yard. My mom moved up to save it just in time.

"Hi, I'm Mrs. Harris and this is Richie. *Say 'hello', Richie.*"

 "Oh...hi." She smiled at me. She was the most beautiful girl I had ever seen.

 "What's your name" my mom asked. I was just standing there breathing out of my mouth.

"Kelly".

"We just wanted to come by and say welcome to the neighborhood. We made you a cake. *Give her the cake now, Richie.*"

I was having trouble with my fine motor skills, but I managed to reach the plate out, so she could take it.

"This looks yummy."

"So, are your parents home. I would love to meet them too."

"My dad is home. I don't know where my mom is."

"Oh, okay. Where are you from?"

"We used to live in California and some other places. We move around..."

"KELLY!"

The voice was startling and made my mom and I take a step back. Kelly shook a little. A huge man stepped into the frame of the front door. He was wet and didn't have a shirt on. He was bigger than Mr. Hearns and even scarier. He had a big beard and a hairy chest.

"Oh, hello. I'm Carol and this is Richie. We live down the street."

The man reached down from the top stair, grabbed Kelly by the arm and pulled her up the stairs toward the doorway. She nearly lost the cake as he she flew up the stairs. It slid into her chest and some of the chocolate frosting got on her shirt.

"We wanted to welcome you to the neighborhood."

I sensed a little fear in my mom's voice. The man hadn't even noticed the cake. He looked down and pushed the cake back off Kelly's shirt. He wiped some of the frosting off her with his hand and licked it off his fingers.

"That's very nice. Thank you."

He picked Kelly up and placed her inside the house. The man turned and looked out at us. There was an uncomfortable pause. It was somehow more uncomfortable than the rest of the uncomfortable conversation to that point.

"Well, it was nice to meet you both. Maybe we can have dinner together someday".

"Yeah...that would be great", the man said. He was closing the door as he said it. Just like that the house seemed uninhabited again.

"She was nice. She might be on the school bus with you. Maybe you can be friends."

"Yeah. Can we go to the store and get some new clothes, Mom."

"What's wrong with the clothes you got?"

New Routine

The next morning, I woke up before the alarm clock, which was a first for me. I got up before my parents and was showered and almost ready for school before they even woke up. I found some cologne that my Dad hadn't opened yet and applied about a quart of it from my face down to my feet. I smelled great if you were standing at least 20 feet away. If you were any closer than that, it was unbearable. My mom woke up and immediately started sneezing.

"What is that??? Oh, my God. Did an Aqua Velva factory explode??"

"I used some of Dad's cologne. Do I smell good?"

"Have you ever heard the phrase *'too much of a good thing'*? No. No, you don't smell good, and you can't go to school like this."

Before I knew it, she had me by the kitchen sink with my shirt off and was washing my upper body down with a wet washcloth.

"Mom! Mom, c'mon! You're going to wash all the cologne off."

"I don't think that's possible, Richie. I think you're going to smell like a middle-aged man for the rest of your life. You can't use that much cologne. Just a little bit is all you need."

"Are we starting a new morning routine?"

"You need to teach your son how to use cologne."

"Did we just skip right by the deodorant lesson?"

"I used some of your deodorant too, Dad. Please tell her how good I smell."

"Oh, yeah. You smell terrific. I just hope nobody in town is allergic to menthol. That was a gift from Grandma. Didn't you notice it was still in the plastic? There's a reason it wasn't opened."

"So, you don't think I smell good?"

"I think if you're going to use that much cologne every day, I am going to need a second job, and you will need to go to school in a hazardous materials suit."

My mom finished sanitizing my upper body. She made me take off the rest of my clothes and immediately put them in the washing machine. My dad spent a few minutes demonstrating the proper application of fragrances and deodorant. He did so while applying them both on himself since I had already put on enough on for a decade. He told me to try to keep my distance from anyone I liked while at school that day.

I ran out to the bus stop as soon as I could. It was way too early, so I was the only one there for a while. After a few minutes, the Simpsons got dropped off by their Mom as they did every day. They were twins, but they weren't the kind that look alike. Billy and Marie Simpson were both nice, but their mom was the worst driver in history. She would always run at least one wheel onto the curb when she stopped to let them out. If it was garbage day, she usually knocked over a can or two as she pulled up. We all knew to back up toward the Towney's front lawn when we saw her car, so we weren't run over. Scott Towney was in my class too. He would always joke about the twins needing helmets when they drove with their mom. That day his jokes were focused on me.

"What's that smell? Is that you, Richie? Did you sleep in your grandparent's bed last night? It smells like old people and mints."

Scott Towney was a jerk. I was pretty sure he would be one for all his life. His level of jerkness just doesn't fade over the years. It seemed to be chronic and at least partly genetic. There were five boys in the Towney family, and each one was a jerk. Scott was the youngest. Their dad was a jerk too. My parents didn't like him. They never said so publicly, but I could tell. Mrs. Towney was a nice lady. I'm not sure how she dealt with all those jerks in the same house.

A few more kids made their way to the bus stop. Each had the same question as they arrived.

"What is that?"

"Richie. He's got a hot date with Mrs. Warren."

Mrs. Warren was our social studies teacher. She was a good teacher, but carbon dating estimated her age at approximately 157 years old. If the classroom ws quiet enough, there was a better than even chance she would fall asleep at her desk.

The unusual scent circling the bus stop that morning prompted each kid to ask what it was as they arrived. Each time Scott, or someone else in the band of jerkwagons who spent their day worshipping him as their leader, would make a different joke about me. Most days the comments would get to me. Not that day. I was preoccupied with waiting for Kelly. I was trying to play it cool, but I couldn't stop looking down the block waiting for her to come out of her house. I was hoping she would want to sit next to me on the bus and in all our classes. I was planning on being her guide around the school and helping her get to know how stuff worked. I basically wanted to spend every waking moment with her since I saw her the day before...I was in total seventh-grade stalker mode.

"Hi."

Brian O'Grady would be picked next. Brian would always be the last kid to arrive at the school because his mom would take him to daily mass every day in the summer. I wasn't sure, if given my choice of punishments, whether I would wear Raji's shoes all summer or go to daily mass with Brian and Mrs. O'Grady. We all figured Mrs. O'Grady must have done something horrible to feel like she had to go to mass every single day. Only really old people who were trying to get into heaven did that. Scott would give Brian a hard time about it. He would joke that Mrs. O'Grady must be running from the cops in Ireland and that's why they moved to the US. Brian would say that Scott's breath smelled like 'shite' and call him a 'ballocks'. I loved that Scott was getting shot down in what was essentially two different languages every day. I liked the way Brian talked. I thought his accent was cool and that it was great learning European curse words. Brian always wanted to play soccer. He was great at it. It wasn't our favorite sport – that was baseball. On the rare occasion when we did play soccer, Brian dominated. He did things to that ball using his feet that Raji and I struggled to do with our hands.

Tommy Howe would get picked after Brian. This meant that Tommy was just slightly more athletic than Raji and I, but he acted like he was god's gift to sports. He was always giving Raji and I a hard time if we blew a play, meanwhile he typically made as many mistakes as either of us. Tommy had to come the longest distance of any of us to get to the school. He lived in a rough part of town. Our whole town was kinda rough, but Tommy's place was in the worst section.

Tommy's dad left his family just after Tommy was born, so it was just Tommy, his mom, and his older brother Kenny. Kenny was a star athlete. He was kind of a town icon. Every once in a while, he would come by and shoot some baskets with us. He was super tall and was able to dunk. That gave him god-like status in our eyes. He had his own car too. It was Dodge Dart, and it looked like the vehicle equivalent of Jimmy's bike. There were all sorts of mismatched parts on it. I guess you would say it was beige though it was tough to tell just what color made up the largest percentage of the car. We didn't care. We were enamored with the idea of having our own cars someday and the freedom it represented. We were all waiting for whatever magic it was that made Kenny so good at sports to happen to Tommy. We were hoping that he would wake up one day and be as good as his brother. I think Tommy assumed it already happened. It didn't. He clearly thought he was the 12-year-old version of Kenny. He talked like it was true. Tommy was the only kid in our crew that went to Wilson. He didn't like the kids there very much though, so he hung out with us.

That was us. That was our crew. It was the same just about every day in the summer. We would get to the school in the morning and play all day until dinner time. We would pick it back up after dinner and head home when the streetlights came on. I hated being the weak link sports wise, but I loved those summers. I didn't realize just how much I loved them until they were gone. There's not much that I wouldn't give up now to jump on a bike and meet the crew at the school today.

The best days were when a group from some other part of town would make the trip to the school and challenge us. We gave each other a hard time, but when some other bunch showed up, it brought us together and you could see how tight we really were. We were tough to beat at any game. Having Terry and Scott was a huge advantage. Those two guys were better than the best kids from any other crew in town. Sometimes the other kids would laugh about us having a girl play with us. That was until Marie ran through them for a touchdown or hit one over their heads. It was usually at that point that you could see their moods change as all the hope they had before the game started to evaporate. It was usually a beat down for whomever dared to show up at the school that day. We would crush most other crews pretty bad. Sometimes it was ugly. Some crews couldn't get a single basket or a touchdown on us, or even so much as two runs in six innings of baseball. Sometimes they would surrender after a game or two and suggest we mix the teams up, so it would be a fairer contest. By far our favorite thing though was when they would just walk slowly and silently back to their bikes and load their equipment up for the 'ride of shame' back to whichever part of town they were from. We would be giving it to them pretty good especially if they were talking a lot of smack before we crushed them. We would all follow a few steps behind them out to the corner and give them a big wave as they left. I loved talking smack. It was great being part of the winning side even though I typically didn't have very much to do with our success.

On hot days we would go swimming in the Simpson's or the Towney's pool. They were the only two families around that had pools. The Simpson's pool was a used above-ground pool that some relative gave them when they upgraded to an in-ground pool. It was small and the filter was always breaking, but we didn't care. It kept us cool and we had fun in it. We almost always swam at the Simpsons even though the Towneys had a bigger pool. Mr. Towney built their pool. He borrowed one of the mini front loaders from where he worked and dug a big hole in the backyard. He got a pool liner from somewhere and threw it in the hole and filled it up with water. It wasn't ideal. There were always leaks to patch and it looked like the hole Mr. Towney dug started to cave in on one end, so the pool was narrower at one end than the other.

We would only swim at the Towneys if Scott's older brothers weren't home, or if Mrs. Towney was there to protect us. If Scott's older brothers were there, and Mrs. Towney wasn't, it wasn't much fun. Scott's older brothers were brutal. They loved launching us into the pool and would compete to see who could throw us the highest and the furthest. One of their favorite physical tortures was to hold us right at the edge of the water as one of the brothers would take a running start and tackle us into the pool. That was a lot of fun. If they weren't doing that, they were holding our heads under water. If Mrs. Towney was there, she didn't allow Scott's brothers in the pool when we were swimming. It was nice when she was there. Mr. Towney had no issue with the medieval pool practices of his oldest sons. He would park a lawn chair on the side of the pool, smoke a cigar, and drink a beer while laughing at it all. It was all just 'boys being boys' to him. It felt closer to 'boys being slowly drowned'. When they finished with us, we would all crawl out of the pool and lay in the grass for a while - battered, exhausted, and clearing water from our lungs.

Every summer day that year was pretty much the same except for one change. As I made my way back from the school or from swimming at the Simpson's or the Towney's house, I always made a point to slow down and cross the street, so I could ride past Kelly's house. I was hoping to catch a glimpse of her and maybe even a chance to talk to her some more. She was a complete ghost ever since the day I met her. Terry would always ride home from the school with me since he lived next door. He was confused and getting frustrated by how slow I would go as we approached Kelly's house, so I had to finally tell him what the deal was.

"There's a really hot girl living in the old Cody house. Her name is Kelly. I met her a few weeks ago, but I haven't seen her since. I was hoping she would come out some day, so I could talk to her."

"I figured that was it. I saw her once too."

"What...when did you see her?"

"I think it was the night they moved in. I saw that van pull up and she got out with her dad and they went in the house. I couldn't see them good cause it was dark, but I figured she was hot because of how you've been staring at the house like a stalker ever since they got here. I haven't seen either of them since that night."

"It's weird, right? Why doesn't she ever come outside."

Terry face got serious for a second. He was kind of amused by my Kelly obsession before that.

"I don't know. I hope nothing bad is happening to her."

"Bad like what? "

"I don't know. Let's go. She's not coming out today. You think your mom will let me sleep over tonight?"

Sleepovers were a big deal back then. It was a bigger deal for my parents who got very little sleep if I had a friend sleep over. Terry would sleep over a lot in the summer. We would stay up forever playing Atari and horsing around. My mom would allow it about half the time we asked her. It depended on if she 'was in any shape to deal with us all night'. Her worked three days a week, and the job required long hours on her feet. Some days she would announce on getting home from work that she "would like to take off her legs and throw them in the corner". I knew those nights were not going to be sleepover nights.

I rarely slept over at Terry's. His mom was a nurse and had to work a lot of nights. Terry's mom was great. She always made the coolest snacks for us when we were there, and she always had a cool art activity or something fun to do inside when it rained. Terry's dad died before he moved to the neighborhood. Terry never talked much about his dad, but I could tell that he missed him a lot. On the nights when Terry's mom had to work, his Uncle John would come over and stay at their place. I liked his Uncle John. He was really cool. He would take us to the boardwalk sometimes and play video games with us at the arcade. He was one of those adults that would put his hand on top of your head and mess up your hair when he saw you. Terry hated when he did that. He would always smack his hand away.

Right before we were going to start riding home, Chris Towney pulled up in front of Kelly's house. Chris was the oldest of the Towney brothers. He got his driver's license a few weeks before. He had already taken down the family's mailbox backing his dad's car out of the driveway, and the rumor was he hit a police car from behind at a stop light downtown. He was delivering pizzas that summer for Angelo's. He got out of the car with a pizza and looked down the street to where we were standing with our bikes. He made a face at us and yelled "what are you dorks looking at".

I had the distinct taste of chlorine in my mouth. Chris yelling at us would usually be enough for me to ride away. I wasn't moving until I saw if Kelly was going to answer the door. Chris turned and made his way up the walk. As he did, someone reached through the blinds in the front window and made some space in order to look outside. My heart was nearly jumping out of my chest as the front door started to open. It seemed like the whole thing was happening in slow motion. Chris got to the front door as it was opening. Kelly's dad stepped halfway out and handed Chris some money. Kelly's dad shaved his beard off and his hair had changed from black to blond, but he was still just as scary as the first time I saw him. He grabbed the pizza and went back inside. There was no sign of Kelly anywhere. The door closed and Chris started back toward his car. He drove past where we were standing and gave us the finger.

"C'mon. She's not coming out."

Terry got back on his bike and started toward his house. I stood there a few seconds hoping for a miracle. A hand pulled the blinds down again, but this time it was the window closest to where I was standing. I nearly jumped out of my skin. I turned around and tripped over my bike. My foot got caught in the spokes. The blinds were still open, and someone was still watching as I struggled to get my foot free. It felt like it was taking forever. I was tearing some of the skin off my ankle trying to wrench my foot out the wheel.

I couldn't feel any pain. All I could think of was that scary man coming out of his house, grabbing me up, and bringing me inside. I would never see anyone ever again. After what felt like an hour, I got free from the spokes. I peddled home as fast as I could. As I got in the front gate, the pain around my foot became a reality. There was a small blood stain on my sock. I hadn't even noticed, but I must have slid right out of my sneaker as I got free of my bicycle spokes. It was probably sitting by the curb down the block near Kelly's house. I wasn't going back to get it even though I had no idea how I was going to explain what happened to my parents. My parent's wrath was not as scary as whatever Kelly's dad would do to me if he got his hands on me.

"Hey, Champ. How was your day?"

"It was fine. Everything is fine. Why do you ask?", I said trying and failing miserably not to arouse any suspicion.

"Just wanted to know. Me and you mom care about you."

"I care about you. I care about you a lot. I'm going to the bathroom now."

"Ok. Thanks for the head's up on that."

My parents had to be a little suspicious about what was going on. I hurried into the bathroom and pulled off my socks. I wiped off the blood from my foot with my not blood-stained sock ensuring that they both had hard-to-remove blood stains. I ran the water and tried cleaning the bicycle chain grease off my leg mindlessly committing what was a major offense in our house: the soiling of my mom's show towels. Even my dad got in trouble for defiling our show towels. We didn't have much money, but we had show towels. It really didn't fit us, but my mom insisted on having them for some reason. Just getting them wet was a punishable offense. My mom did an inspection of the bathroom each time I used it. The show towel status was paramount to the process. This situation was very bad. The thought crossed my mind to flush my socks and the show towels, but the thought of Todd with his foot in the toilet in the girl's locker room ran across my mind. I didn't want to try to explain a clogged toilet to my parents as water and whatever else flowed out under the bathroom door. I could jump in the shower and wash the blood and grease off myself as well as my socks and the show towels. That would raise suspicion as I had never to that point taken a shower once school ended without a direct parental order. I crunched the numbers processing every possible option for resolving my conundrum through the robust organic data-analytics engine inside my then 12-year-old head. After carefully analyzing the situation and weeding through all the possible outcomes, there remained only two realistic options: I could throw my socks and the show towels out of the bathroom window denying any knowledge as to their current whereabouts or any awareness of the circumstances leading up to their inevitable discovery outside the house, or I could I tell the truth. I could level with my parents about Kelly; about jamming my foot inside my bike spokes; about bleeding on my sock; about leaving my sneaker on the street; about trying to clean myself up with my other sock and my mom's sacred show towels; about everything. I could throw myself on the mercy of the court and beg for forgiveness vowing never to do anything like this again. Just these two options remained.

I made my choice and emerged from the bathroom confidently. This was clearly the best option and would lead to the best possible outcome for me from what was a nearly untenable situation. I was proud of myself for thoroughly analyzing the options and making the best possible decision. I walked into the living room to address my parents.

"Hey, Buddy, why did you leave a sneaker on your handlebars?"

"What?"

"Dad went out to put your bike in the garage and your sneaker was hanging on the handlebars."

A chill ran up my spine. I was frozen. Everything I had planned to say vaporized in an instant. I was speechless save for one word.

"Sneaker?"

"Yes, you've heard of sneakers, right? You left a sneaker hanging off your bike. It's still there. No big deal – just wondering why?"

It would have been an innocuous exchange except for how weird I was making the whole situation. I couldn't help it. I was lost in the thought of Kelly's dad walking outside to get my sneaker and carrying it down the block to our house. He had *my* sneaker in his hand and walked into *my* yard in front of *my* house and hung it on *my* bike. This was clearly a message. He was trying to tell me something. It was a direct threat. He was delivering a warning: stay away or suffer the consequences. My parents, who had really thought nothing of the situation until their simple question left me speechless and paralyzed in fear in the middle of the living room, now stood up to shake me out of it. They walked me out the front door to the garage. My dad opened the door, and there it was. My bike was right in the front with some slightly bent spokes and my left sneaker dangling off the handlebars by the laces. I was in shock.

"It's no big deal. Why are you acting so weird?"

I still had no response. I was fixated on the sneaker and what it meant. I just shrugged and mumbled a bit in response to their questions. They were exasperated at why I couldn't explain this simple seemingly meaningless detail. After a few seconds my mom caught sight of something on the side of our house.

"ARE THOSE MY TOWELS?"

Grounded

There's not much worse than being grounded in the summertime. It's bad during the school year too, but during school it's just a few hours from the time you get home from school until it's time to go to bed. In the summer, every minute of the day is agony. You look out the window and see other kids your age outside. That is the worst. - It actually burns watching them having fun. You can feel it burning in your chest. And the weather – why is it that the best weather days were always the days when I was grounded?? It's a scientific fact. If people only knew how it worked, they would pay my parents to ground me because it would ensure that those days would be the nicest days of the year. It never rained when I was grounded. Not once. Not ever. Not a drop. Every day I was grounded was a day filled with radiant sunshine and gentle breezes. I swear I would see people outside on the days that I was grounded who never left the house otherwise. It was that nice. The second day I was on lockdown for the show towels incident, I looked out the front window in the morning after I got up, and there they were: Mr. and Mrs. Chapman walking down the street in front of my house with their old dog, Butch. They never left the house. Never. The government must have air lifted supplies down the chimney, so they could survive. I had honestly thought that all three of them died years earlier. Butch was so old that my dad had more hair on his back than Butch had left on his body. Mrs. Chapman had one real leg and one poorly made fake leg. I think Mr. Chapman made the fake leg in his garage probably because they didn't want to leave the house to pick up a proper prosthetic leg. Mrs. Chapman was so inspired by the weather that she wasn't even using her cane that day. Mr. Chapman lost one eye in a bar fight when he was in his twenties. He had an eye patch. We all called him 'The Pirate'. It was obvious that The Pirate had given up on combing his hair or really any form of personal hygiene decades earlier. There was no reason to bother with cleaning yourself up if you aren't going to leave the house. The Chapmans car went on fir- a few years earlier, and they still didn't come outside. The fire department came and put the fire out, but not before the car was destroyed. The whole neighborhood was there to watch the event, but not the Chapmans. The fire chief had to knock on the door to let them know that the fire was out, and they were leaving now. The burned-out car was still in their yard. But today – today was so incredibly beautiful outside that even this small band of hermits couldn't resist. Honestly the Loch Ness monster was sighted more often than the Chapmans. But there they were, walking right by our house. Such was the weather when I was grounded. They saw me standing there dejectedly looking out the front window. They waved at me and smiled as they sipped sweet tea. It was hard to take especially since both of my parents worked. Going outside to play with my crew was a constant temptation. I knew what time my mom and dad got home every day. I just needed to get back a few minutes before them. My mom convinced me that she had spotters planted all over the neighborhood though. If I stepped one foot outside the house, my life would be over. I would be stuck in the house until senior prom. It worked. I never left – not even once. Years later my mom admitted it wasn't true. She just told me that people were watching me, so I would stay inside. There was that burning sensation again.

I emerged from lockdown after what felt like a year but was probably just a few days in reality. If you check with the National Weather service, you'll see it was overcast and rainy that day. My release coincided with Todd's. When I got to the school that day, Todd was there. It was the first time he was allowed outside since he got caught in the girls' locker room that day. Everyone was giving Todd a hard time about the failure of his plan. It was the typical lighthearted stuff any of us would get after we got grounded or did something stupid. We had all forgotten that Marie was on the softball team. She was in the locker room that day when Todd got his foot stuck in the toilet. She wasn't amused at all.

"STOP IT. IT'S NOT FUNNY. IT'S DISGUSTING."

We were all shocked. Marie was very soft spoken. I don't think any of us had heard her yell before that day. Everyone just kind of stopped for a second as we realized why she was upset. She was always one of the guys to all of us, and she was one of the guys in almost every way. I think that was the first day any of us understood that she wasn't one of the guys in *every* way. It should have been something that clicked for us a long time before that. Todd tried to apologize, but Marie wasn't having any of it. He was pleading with her not to leave and telling her how sorry he was. Marie got on her bike and was gone. I started thinking about all the crude language and dumb jokes we made while she was around. I felt stupid and sorry. We all did. We just stood there quiet and watched her ride away. Everyone was silent for a little while after she left. She didn't come back to hang out with us again that summer. Todd would always check with Billy to see if he told her that Todd was sorry. He said that he did, but Marie never really had any response. Billy told us that she found another crew to hang with in the next town. It felt bad that she didn't want to be part of our crew anymore. We didn't talk about it, but we all missed her.

It took about three weeks for us to learn exactly how much we missed Marie. That was the day she rode up to the school with her new friends. We had never seen these guys before. They were from the next town over. They were bigger than us. They had nicer bikes, and they had much better equipment. I would be lying if I said we weren't a little intimidated when they showed up at the school. This wasn't going to be the usual beat down. I couldn't look away as they warmed up. None of us could. Everything they did was perfect. I was trying to find a weak player, and I couldn't. It seemed like they were a team of all-stars. We were all kind of mesmerized. They looked like the Yankees out there. Marie too. She was even better than I remembered. She was super focused too. I was hoping to make eye contact with her to give her a friendly wave, but she never looked our way. Not once. Scott spoke up and broke the trance we were all in.

Scott started racing toward right field immediately at the crack of the bat. It was standard operating procedure for whomever was in center field. The center fielder would sprint toward right field as fast as humanly possible and try to bail me out on fly balls. If they stayed in the air long enough, the center fielder would make the catch in right field. If not, they would chase down the inevitably misplayed ball and relay it into the infield as quickly as possible. The same protocol was followed by our first and second basemen. They each turned and went into a dead sprint toward where I was standing in right field. There was no way Scott or anyone else was going to make it in time. This ball was hit way too hard. I was going to miss it, Marie was going to score, and we were going to lose. I always struggled with fly balls. They were a mystery to me. I didn't know how other kids could tell where they were going to land. I would never be anywhere close to where the ball would finally fall out of the sky. I had a better chance of finding gold in the grass in right field than of ever catching a fly ball. The good news on that day was that it wasn't a fly ball. It was a line drive. It was the hardest hit ball that day by a mile. I really didn't have to move very much. In fact, I hardly needed to move at all. It was hit right at me. I mean right at me. It was coming *right at me. It's coming right at me! Oh, shit!* I turned my body around and put my right hand right behind my glove. It was kind of like I was trying to command the ball to halt. I should have stayed in teacup position.

'Ughhhh!'

It was an involuntary guttural sound that came from the ball impacting my stomach and forcing all the air in my body up through my esophagus and out of my mouth at high speed. The impact launched me backward off my feet and onto my back. The pain in my midsection was more intense than any pain I had experienced in my life to that point. Scott made it over to the crash site first. I assumed he would start first aid and alert first responders, but he had other concerns.

"Where is the damn ball? RICHIE, WHERE IS THE BALL??

"What? I don't know. I'm bleeding internally here."

Scott scanned the entire area, but the ball was nowhere in sight.
He pulled back my hands from where I was covering up my battered
torso. There it was. The ball must have rolled into my glove after it
hit me in the belly. It never touched the ground. Scott grabbed it
and raised it up over his head. Up to that point, nobody could tell if
it was a hit.

"He caught it! He friggin caught it."

He was showing the other team and the rest of the kids in the
infield. Marie had taken a few steps down the line fully expecting
me to miss the ball allowing her to walk home and score. She raced
back toward third base to tag up. Scott pulled the ball down and
hurled it into the infield. Our first and second baseman had raced
into the outfield, according to our team's established best practices
when the ball was hit to me in right field. The ball hit right near
second base and started rolling slowly toward the pitcher's mound.
Terry raced to the ball as Marie neared the plate. Terry turned and
fired a rocket to Todd who was catching. Todd turned with the ball
just as Marie arrived at the plate. Marie had no intention of sliding.
This was back in the good ol' days when you could run over the
catcher at home plate. Marie hit Todd like a Mack truck at full
speed. Todd, the ball, his catcher's mitt, his facemask, and anything
that wasn't strapped tightly to his body went in multiple directions
behind home plate. Marie scored. 1-0 visitors.

Raji just shook his head and took a drink out of his canteen. Yeah, he started bringing an actual canteen with him on the days he came to the school. He was covered if we ever got lost in one of the many deserts in New Jersey.

"I am performing at my current best level of capabilities, Scott. If this is not sufficient you can excommunicate me from the ball team."

Excommunicate? There was always a better than even chance that we wouldn't understand some of the words Raji used when he spoke. His vocabulary was just more advanced than ours. As he got upset, the number of unfamiliar terms he used would rise exponentially.

"I think everyone had enough today. Nice work, guys."

Terry mercifully ended our activities that night. We were all thankful to be spared from Coach Todd's wrath before heat exhaustion set in. I don't blame Scott for how he was after we lost. His dad used to make Scott and his brothers run when they lost games. It didn't matter the sport. If they lost a game, you could find them running laps around their house or sprinting in their backyard. Mr. Towney hated losing. The drills wouldn't stop until his sons were laying on the ground exhausted, or Mrs. Towney came out and put a stop to things. I think Scott just thought it was normal. It wasn't normal.

It was just about time to go anyway. Todd had already left as he couldn't afford to push things with his dad at home carefully watching the clock. He always left a few minutes before anyone else to be sure he didn't get home late. As soon as Terry and I started peddling toward home, Terry's bike made a weird sound. We stopped for a second and then tried to go again, but his bike wouldn't work. Jimmy came over and crouched next to Terry's bike and started looking things over.

"I see what's wrong. Hop off for a second."

Two full and complete sentences from Jimmy. It was the most he spoke all summer. Terry hopped off as Jimmy started playing with the chain and gears, or whatever he was doing. It was a mystery to Terry and me. If it wasn't for Jimmy, I think most of us would be walking wherever we wanted to go.

"I have to be home soon. Do you think you can fix it quick or should I just walk it?"

"Yeah, it shouldn't take long."

"I'm gonna get going, so I'm not late."

"Ok. Later."

I started for home. It was really hot, and I was really tired. I was sweating as much as I had at any point that summer. Sweat dripped from under my hat down my face. It was hard to keep it out of my eyes and mouth. It burned a little and the salty taste got into my mouth. I was using one hand to steer my bike while the other constantly wiped the sweat away. August was a good month because it was summer, but it was always the hottest and most humid part of the year. When the calendar hit August, I also started to feel a little bit anxious. It's the *last* month of summer, and it meant school was starting soon. It felt like a Sunday night does when you know you have to work on Monday. You just wanted the clock to stop so you could squeeze out as much fun as possible. It never did. August is like a month of Sunday nights. It always felt like one of the fastest months of the year just because you wished it wasn't. It was like trying to remember a dream. The more I would try to remember, the more it would slip away.

I had stopped crossing over to the other side of the street to ride in front of Kelly's house on my way home. It seemed pointless. I hadn't seen her since the week she moved in. If it wasn't for the van in the driveway, there was nothing that indicated there was anyone living in the house. The van was now pulled up almost into the backyard. The front wheels and most of the car was in the grass at the side of the house. Only the rear wheels and the back of the van were still in the driveway. It was like they were expecting company and wanted to give them as much room as possible to fit their cars in. If you looked really quick, you wouldn't even see there was a van there, and you would swear the house was vacant.

At night there didn't even appear to be any lights on inside. I had all but given up on the remote chance of seeing Kelly on the way home. I would slow down a bit and stare at the house as I went by, but I didn't bother riding onto the other side of the street like I did earlier that summer. Terry was pleased as he was getting frustrated with me always slowing so much in front of the house. I stopped in part because it seemed pointless, but I was also scared of her dad. I knew there was just as much of a chance that I could run into him as Kelly on any given night. I got the message he sent me with the 'sneaker incident'. I was pretty sure if I needed to, I could get away from him on my bike if he tried to get me as long as I was on the other side of the street. I wasn't so sure I could escape if I was on the same side.

"Richie."

I definitely heard someone say my name, but I couldn't tell where it was coming from.

"Richie."

That time it was louder. It was coming from the hedges along the side of the Mercer's house. The Mercers lived across the street from Kelly. They were an older couple whose children had moved out a long while ago. I was just past their house when I heard my name. I turned my bike around and cautiously peddled a little back toward the front of the Mercer's place. I was afraid it was some kind of trick by Kelly's dad. I wasn't taking any chances. As I got to walkway of the Mercer's, I could see her. She was kneeling in the hedges looking out toward the street where I was on my bike. I couldn't believe it. I was frozen there for a second. Well, maybe it was more than a second. She had to shake me out of my daze.

"Come here! Hurry!"

I couldn't move fast enough. I just about tripped over myself just setting the kick stand down on my bike. I raced to where she was hiding in the hedges and crouched down beside her. The verbal diarrhea started almost immediately.

"Hey, what are you doing here? How come you never come outside? We play at the school almost every day. You should come and play with us. It's fun. We play all kinds of stuff – baseball, basketball, football, even soccer sometimes. Do you have a bike? It's not far. You could ride there in a few minutes. I can give you a ride on my bike if you don't have a bike. I don't mind. Are you going to go to St. Ann's this year? What grade are you in? Are you going to go to Woodrow Wilson? I have friends there too. It would be cool if you went to St. Ann's though. You should tell your dad you want to go to St. Ann's. We would be on the bus together. We could sit together. I could show you around and introduce you to everyone. Where are you from? Where is your mom? Is you dad mean to you? How come I never see you? Does he not let you play outside?"

It was amazing that I could pose so many questions in such a short time. There was no way anyone listening could have processed it all. Kelly didn't even look at me as I was rambling. I wasn't sure if she was listening. She never turned away from the center of the Mercer's backyard. I'm pretty sure I could have rattled off a few more minutes of disconnected pre-teen nervous stream-of-consciousness babble, but she reached out without looking and put her hand on mine. It stopped me cold.

"Look."

I couldn't see what she was looking at. It was an average backyard. There was nothing notable about it. The Mercer's had a shed. It was a shed like any other shed. There was a tree in the middle of the yard. They had a bird bath under the tree, but there weren't any birds it that night. There was a rake and a shovel standing against the back fence. They had one of those old-school mowers where the blades spin as you push it. That was also sitting there against the back fence next to the rake and shovel. There was nothing remarkable about any of it. I couldn't understand what she was so fixated by.

"What? What are you looking at? I don't see anything."

She squeezed my hand. It was the highlight of my young life looking down at her hand holding mine. I felt it all over – not just my hand. It was magic. I looked up at her as she looked into the distance. I had never seen anything so beautiful. Everything about her was perfect. I wanted her to look at me, but she was still staring into the yard.

"Look at them. They light up."

She pointed toward the center of the yard. I wasn't sure how I missed them. It was like they weren't there until she said it. There was a swarm of lightning bugs under the tree. Those of us who grew up here hardly noticed them anymore. They came out almost every night in the late summer. There was a novelty to them when we were younger. I remember my mom showing me lightning bugs for the first time. I wasn't keen on bugs, so she held my hand as we walked into a small group of them that were dancing around in our backyard. She reached out and one landed on her hand. She gently brought it toward me and let it walk into my palm. It stayed for a bit lighting up bright against the dark night before it flew off. As we got older, we stopped noticing. We got focused on whatever it was we were doing, and the light never seemed to catch our eye again. They just kind of faded into the background of our lives. I realized that this was the first time Kelly had ever seen them. It made me take notice again. They were amazing. I was remined how special they are after not even noticing them for years. I watched her watching them light up the night for a few seconds at a time. After a bit, I ran out to the center of the yard and cupped one in my hands. I brought it back to where Kelly was sitting in the hedges.

"Here."

"It's okay? They don't sting?"

"No, it's okay. They don't sting."

I let it walk into her hands. It lit up bright in the darkness of the hedges. Off then on and off again. I watched it for a second, but there was so much more to watching her watching it. The light radiated against her sitting there in the dark hedges. I remember how the light glimmered in her eyes and the way she sat there so still and content. It must have felt how she marveled at it, and how it couldn't have been safer anywhere else in the world. After a while it lifted off her hands and returned to where the others were under the tree.

"I can get another one. You could take it home and keep it in a jar.
It can be yours. Then you can watch it light up all the time."

I was about to run out into the yard to grab another one for her
when she took my hand again.

"No. We shouldn't keep them in a jar. They're happy outside.
That's probably why they light up – because they're happy."

It seemed weird to me – the idea of a bug being happy or sad, but I
liked the thought of them lighting up because they were happy.
She kept staring out at them with her hand in mine. I could have
stayed there all night with her. It was like we were the only people
in the world. She watched for a few minutes in silence; then
jumped up to her feet. She turned and looked at me.

"I wish I could come and play, but I'm not allowed. I used to have a
bike, but I don't anymore. I don't know if I'm going to St. Ann's, but
I'd like to sit with you on the bus. I don't know where my mom is
now. I think she's still in California. I have to go now."

She sprinted away across the street into the backyard of her house
and disappeared. I stood there dumbfounded by what just
happened. I had so many more questions. I wanted to stay there
watching the lightning bugs with her all night. I was frozen there at
the front of the Mercer's house for a minute just processing it all. It
was a staggering few minutes. She listened to me. She actually
heard me and responded. She knew I was there. I was important.
And – she held my hand. *She held my hand*. I couldn't get over how
she reached out to me and squeezed my hand.

"What's the story? You trying to burn the place down with your
eyes."

Terry got his bike going thanks to Jimmy and pulled up next to me in front of the Mercer's house.

"She was out here. She held my hand."

"Cool. What did she say?"

'What? Umm...She said she didn't know if she is going to St. Ann's and her mom is in California."

"That sounds like an interesting conversation – weird, but interesting. You gonna stand out here all night?"

As we got closer to my house, I recognized my Uncle Bill's car in the driveway. Terry's Uncle John's car was in his driveway. He was sitting on the porch waiting for Terry to get home. He stood up and waved at us as we got closer.

"You think I can stay over tonight?"

"I can ask but My Uncle and Aunt are over. She always says no when we have company."

I ran in the house and asked, but it went as expected. I walked back out to give Terry the news.

"She said no. We got family visiting. I'll see you tomorrow?"

Terry shoulders sunk a bit dejected by the news.

"Yeah, see you tomorrow."

I turned to walk into the house, undoubtedly to hear about whatever awesome things my cousin was doing.

"Hey, Richie! I'm glad she held your hand."

Group bike rides always meant fart competitions. To be honest, farts were a standard part of any day, whether we were riding somewhere or not. It was always acceptable to interrupt the action and let one loose. But bike rides were especially gaseous occasions. I'm not sure if it was the combination of our love of highly processed junk food and the vibration of a bike ride, but there would be cacophony of gastrointestinal blasts any time we took formation for a ride. There were always way more sound effects per hour on a bike ride than during any other activity. There was always someone calling for quiet as they stood up on their bike pedals, angled their rear ends out, and ripped one as loudly as possible. Usually the competitor would introduce the act with a loud "I got one!" We would rate them like it was an Olympic event. The scoring was primarily based on volume and length. The louder and longer a fart was, the funnier it was, and the higher score it would receive. The best scoring farts were long and loud. We would rate them on a scale from 'chick fart' to 10, where 'chick fart' was the worst score, and 10 was the best. The 'chick fart' rating was a tribute to Marie. Marie wasn't a frequent participant in our fart competitions. She found it mildly amusing at best, but once in a great while, she 'chimed in'. She never got very high marks, which I don't think she was too disappointed about.

One of the biggest ongoing debates of our youth was whether the continuation rule should apply to our flatulence scoring system. The 'continuation' rule was a basketball thing. In the NBA, a basket would count if a player was fouled while taking a shot as long as the shot was considered to be one continuous motion to the basket. Half of us were for the continuation rule for fart scoring. Half of us were against it. Those who were for the continuation rule argued that if there were very short breaks between a series of farts they should be scored together since it was a 'continuation' of a single fart. Those against the continuation rule said a fart was one sound from beginning to end and a series of farts had to be scored as separate and distinct events. I'm not sure we ever truly resolved the issue nor if the world cares.

The ride to the game that day was a short one in terms of distance, but it was a world away at the same time. It was hard to believe what a difference a few blocks made. Once we hit Stokes Street, the difference was immediate. It seemed each house was larger than the last one, and each driveway had at least one sports car in it that elicited a chorus of 'oohs' and 'ahs'. I couldn't count the number of times someone said '*look at that one*' as we made our way to the field. Every house had an in-ground pool behind it with some rich kids swimming in it. It was hard to see the backyards over the elaborate fences, but if we stood up on our pedals, you could catch a glimpse of them. The front lawns were like professional baseball infields, and there wasn't any trash along the curbs.

We each had a favorite house. It wasn't something we talked about, but it was there, just below the surface of where we stopped sharing our true feelings with one another. My favorite was a brick ranch at the corner of Thompson and Long. There were very few single-story homes, so I liked that it wasn't like the rest. It just seemed like our family would fit perfectly in it. It wasn't super huge like some of the other houses, but it was by no means small either. It took a while for us to ride our bikes the full length of the property. I liked that there were two identical trees in front of the house on either side of the walkway. There were flower boxes under all the windows with an array of different colors inside. My mom would always talk about putting flower boxes under our windows, but we never did. The driveway had this neat curvy pathway that curled around the back of the house where the garage was. I think it was the first house I saw that had a garage that wasn't right in the front. There was a short white picket fence around the outside of the property. I remembered my mom saying how she thought white picket fences were so nice. I thought of her as we rode by and how I would like to buy that house for her someday. I would make her close her eyes and walk her right between those trees before letting her see the place. I would let her take it all in and ask why we were there before presenting her with the keys. She would probably cry tears of joy as she gave me a huge hug and ran up to the front door. My mom's show towels would fit better in that house, and she would need more since we would have a few bathrooms to decorate. My dad would give me pat on the back and that look he gave me when he was proud. I loved that look.

It got very quiet on that ride after the first few blocks into the neighborhood. I think we were all thinking about ourselves living in those homes and swimming in those pools. Our pace slowed after we got tired of pointing out things to each other. I think everyone was running a similar dream scenario through their minds. Most of us hadn't spent much time outside our own town, but we had driven through neighborhoods like these. None of us had really taken note before. I knew my Uncle Bill and Aunt Tina were well off, but it wasn't a thing before that day. Our excitement at what we were seeing slipped away as we passed each house and was replaced with something else. Something not as innocent. I don't think any of us felt like we weren't rich before that day. We felt the gap between our town and theirs for the first time that day.

The park was amazing. It was immense – there were multiple fields. I counted three baseball fields and we couldn't see all the way through the trees to the other half of the place. They had football fields and soccer fields too. They were separate. It wasn't like most places where they just played both sports on the same field. There were eight basketball courts along one side. Each had all the lines painted on – even the three-point line. All the baskets were straight, and they had nets. The nets on the baskets in our town usually disappeared about two hours after they were put up. There were water fountains everywhere and they all worked perfectly. There was no graffiti anywhere. It seemed like we walked into a sports paradise. There were people running around on a track that looped around the outside of the whole place. There were playgrounds for little kids. A crew of guys with yellow shirts went around on golf carts emptying the trash cans and cutting the grass. There were adults in a small grassy section doing aerobics. I think we all stood there at the entrance for a few minutes just taking it all in.

We recognized Marie and a couple of the kids we played against the week before on one of the baseball fields. It was perfect. There were dugouts and home-run fences in the outfield. Our fields didn't have fences. You got a home run simply by hitting it past the outfielders and sprinting around the bases. And there were bases - not just old shirts or garbage can lids. We parked our bikes in the bike rack on the third base side. We hung our two bats on the bat rack and took turns drinking the cold water from the fountain inside our dugout. Terry walked out to the pitcher's mound and stood on the rubber. It was raised just like the pros. There was even a rosin bag behind the rubber for the pitcher to dry his hands. There were white lines all the way out to two huge foul poles in left and right fields. There were lights on each of the fields. I had never played a night baseball game. It would be cool to come back some night and play. None of us were doing anything baseball related. We were just milling around different parts of the field taking it all in. Once we had seen enough, we made our way over to the first base side where Marie and a few other kids were playing catch.

"When is the rest of your team getting here?"

"The rest of our team?"

"Yeah, when are they supposed to get here?"

"I don't think anybody else is coming."

"What do you mean? We're supposed to play. We talked about it last week."

"I don't think anyone else is coming. It's just us today. Some of the guys are away on vacation. Some of them are at camp."

"What the hell? Camp? They went camping? Like Boy Scout shit?"

"No. Camp. Like sports camp. Football camp, basketball camp. You know...camp."

I had never even heard of such a thing. None of us did. A sports camp...where you slept away from home and just played a sport? That sounded awful to me – just being the worst kid in my own town was enough. I didn't need to suck at some sport for an entire week in front of bunch of strangers. I think Scott was envious that kids got to go to sports camp. I was liking the idea of Boy Scout camping.

"We rode all the way here. What now?"

The kids really didn't respond. They just kept playing catch. They gave Scott a shrug and kept tossing the ball.

"Okay, then you guys forfeit. We win."

"Forfeit? How can you forfeit a game that was never scheduled?" They never stopped playing catch as they seemed nothing more than amused by Scott's distress.

"It was scheduled. We talked about it last week. Somebody on your team said, 'next time we play at our place'. That's here. This is your place, and we are ready to play, and you don't have enough players. You forfeit. You lose. It's 1-1."

The full scope of Scott's idea of this clash of towns came into view as he stood there getting more and more angry. He saw last week's game as part of a much larger series of baseball games that were being tracked on some scoreboard somewhere. It was really just in Scott's mind that this competition existed. The rest of us were just kind of following along. Scott saw this as a seven-game series, and last week's loss was just game one. We were there that day to tie the series at 1-1. These kids clearly did not share even the slightest bit of his view of things. He had somehow rationalized this epic series where we would take turns hosting games until it was finally settled as to which town was better. It was clear to us now that these kids had forgotten the game last week and all of us about five minutes after they left our field. It was worse in Scott's mind that they didn't care. It would somehow be better if we played out this imagined series and lost than to have them not care about it. He was growing livid. His face grew redder by the second.

"Whatever, Dude. Yeah, you win."

We all froze in place. Terry started on a dead sprint from the mound as soon as he heard it. We all knew, but this poor kid had no idea. He had his back to Scott and continued to throw and catch. It was a cardinal rule in the Towney house. The 'W' word was forbidden. One of the worst beatings Scott ever received was when he used the 'W' word in response to his dad giving him a hard time about losing some little league game. Scott had developed a sensitivity to the word from that day on. We couldn't use it anywhere near him even if we weren't talking to him. These poor kids had no idea. Some poor unsuspecting dude just used the forbidden word while directly addressing Scott about a fantasy game that Scott had been obsessing over for days. Scott tossed his glove aside and made a beeline for the kid. He had this face he would make when he was really pissed. It was scary. He had that face on as he moved in on the poor kid.

"Mike!"

Marie knew the W rule and what was coming. She shouted and pointed at Scott as her catch partner had his back to the raging maniac coming his way. The kid turned and just stood there like a tackling dummy with no idea that he was in grave danger. Terry couldn't get there in time.

"WHATEVER?!"

Scott hauled off and nailed the kid with a right cross. The kid didn't so much as take his glove off or get his hands anywhere near his face to defend himself. He went down in a heap. Terry got there to keep any more punches from landing. There would have been more for sure.

"You're such a dick, Scott."

Marie knelt next to her teammate near first base where the world series of Scott Towney's mind was just cancelled. 'Mike' was bleeding from the lip and had some visible tears in his eyes. Marie pulled out a batting glove from the Mike's back pocket and used it to wipe off his face. I remember the batting glove because none of us ever owned one. Rich kids had batting gloves. We had all figured our batting averages would be about 100 points higher if we could just get our hands on a pair. Mike got to his feet and was ready to get it on. His friends fell in behind him and dropped their gloves. We dropped our gloves and fell in behind Scott and Terry. The other kid stopped his advance and his friends did the same. There were a few moments of silence as we sized each other up. There were more of us that day, so they thought better of it, and backed away. Scott was definitely being an asshole that day, and was kind of an asshole in general, but he was *our* asshole. We were a crew and that's just how it goes. Every crew has one dude that might not have been tolerated if circumstances were different. But he was always part of the crew so that's that. We were together no matter what. We were the only ones who could give Scott a hard time. Outsiders couldn't. It just wasn't going to happen, not without going through all of us. Going through me personally posed about as much of a challenge as going through an old screen door, but we did have some tough dudes in our group. Our crew was formidable enough that we didn't really have any scrapes growing up despite there being some tough sections of town, and some guys who seemed to think a fight was as much fun as any other activity that you could engage in.

The two teams separated and soon thereafter our crew was being escorted from the nicest park any of us had ever set foot in. The same guys who were cutting the grass and emptying trash cans, also served as park security. They were emptying some of what must have seemed to them like white trash from their park. There was a police car with its lights on at the entrance of the park. It was the nicest park I had ever been to, and I didn't get a chance to so much as throw a ball or shoot one basket. Not one sport activity – nothing. We were made aware that we were no longer welcome to the park and that we would be receiving the honor of a police escort home. The police car followed closely behind us as we rode in our standard unspoken formation all the way to our side of the imaginary boundary between our two towns. The homes seemed even bigger, the pools more luxurious, and the cars faster and cooler than when we rode past them earlier that day. All of it seemed even further away.

"Kiss my arse, Copper"!

Brian gave the cop a nice sendoff as he turned his car around at the edge of town. We all laughed. That's how the Towney World Series ended. We never played those guys at anything again. I guess the Series ended 1-1 if you bought into Scott's view of things. We lost 2-0 if you didn't.

Hard Lessons

August raced by just like it always did. I dreaded the start of school. The only good news was that I might get to see Kelly again. I spent a lot of time in the bathroom the morning of the first day of eighth grade trying to look as good as possible. Most of that time was spent on my hair. It was always short, and I always combed it the same for as long as I could remember. In reality, my hair looked as good as it was going to after about a minute of work. The rest of the time I spent on it wasn't improving anything. It just felt like I needed to get every hair in place. I had mastered the art of applying cologne over the last few weeks of the summer in preparation for this day. I used just a little more than my dad showed me. I figured he was being conservative, so I needed more to make an impact. After my mom dragged me out of the bathroom, I informed her that I wasn't hungry. The truth was that I was afraid eating breakfast that day might make me look fat. I was about as far from fat as a kid could get. I learned years later that my parents were slipping me high calorie drinks - like you might give an elderly person - out of concern for how skinny I was. I looked a lot like someone put glasses on a flagpole. I was pretty convinced that cereal and toast would go right to my hips, and Kelly might think I was fat, so there was no way I was eating. I wanted to go right from the bathroom to the bus stop in my typical way-too-early fashion. My mom made me make a pit stop in front of the house for pictures. I was less than thrilled, of course. At least my mom did the pictures at our house. Some moms were at the bus stop that day taking shots. That would have been way worse.

"Any sign of her?"

Terry knew exactly where my head was. I didn't need to say anything and didn't try to hide it from him.

"Nothing. The van hasn't moved an inch and she hasn't come out of there."

"Maybe she's going to Wilson. They start later in the morning."

Jimmy came and stood next to us. He had a Walkman in his hand and headphones over his head. It looked like it was busted up at one point and put back together. There was some duct tape visible along one side of the unit. The Walkman itself was bright yellow. The headphones were purple and were clearly not the ones that came with the device, but they seemed to work fine. We could faintly hear a Springsteen song playing as he got close. He gave us a silent head nod hello.

We backed away as Mrs. Simpson drove up with the twins. She bumped the Towney's garbage can as she stopped with the front right tire up on the curb – in her typical fashion. I could hear Billy yell 'MOM' as she rode up onto the curb.

"Oh, relax. I got it. Give me a kiss."

Marie was happy to give her mom a kiss, but it was not so with Billy. We boys were at that age where public displays of affection from our parents weren't cool anymore. Billy's lips barely made contact with his mom's cheek as he tried to rush it as quickly as possible. Everyone was watching. As Mrs. Simpson drove away, the ribbing started immediately.

"Can I have a kiss goodbye too, Billy"

The bus arrived about 30 seconds later. We had a new driver. We were disappointed because Mr. Reilly had been our driver for a few years. He was a nice man. He let us pick the radio station we wanted, and he made some extra stops on the way home that weren't really on the list for kids that had a longer distance between their houses and the official bus stop. Mr. Reilly always seemed happy. He always had a loud 'good morning' for all the kids when they got on the bus.

The new driver was much younger, and he wasn't as nice. Scott asked him where Mr. Reilly was. His response was a terse "I don't know. Go sit down." That was pretty much how any interaction with the new guy went. He had a radio station he liked that he wouldn't change for us. The music wasn't so bad, and it wasn't even that big of an issue that he wasn't nice. There's not really much interaction needed to be a successful school bus driver. The real problems were that he smelled, and he drove too fast. He smelled awful and you could smell him from any seat on the bus. It didn't matter where you were sitting. We all would keep the windows open despite it being cool outside in the morning. It was better to be a little cold than to deal with the odor. Plus, he drove really fast. We were bouncing around a lot more than when Mr. Reilly was our driver. Other drivers would honk a lot at our bus because of the way the new guy was driving. We started calling him 'Stink Racer'. We didn't do this to his face since he looked like he might stab us. But, in private conversations, at a safe distance from the bus, he was known as 'Stink Racer'.

It turned out that Stink Racer had some legal issues. The police were waiting for our bus on the Friday of our first week of school. They took "Stink Racer" off the bus in handcuffs. We weren't told what he did to get arrested. We were asked to say a prayer for him when we got to our classes. I prayed for him – mostly that he would turn his life around and a little that God would help him with his personal hygiene habits. I also prayed for Mr. Reilly to come back. That second part came true. Mr. Reilly was our bus driver for the rest of the school year. The bus was a much more pleasant place to be after that first week.

It became a tradition of mine to start the first day of school each year by stopping into Mr. Wood's room. He wasn't listed as my math teacher that year. Sadly, again I had someone else. I always made a point to stop and see Mr. Woods before classes started on the first day of school and talk with him a bit about the summer. Mr. Wood's usually spent part of his summer volunteering somewhere. He always had some cool stories and pictures from wherever he was. He helped some people in South America build a bridge across a river one year. His pictures from that trip were especially cool because the Harlem Globetrotters visited while he was there. He got some neat pictures with the team and got to play basketball with them. He was sure to explain that the bridge was the major accomplishment, rather than shooting hoops with the Globetrotters. It was hard for me to pretend to be as excited about the bridge pictures as I was about his pictures with the Globetrotters.

He would always tell me about something he learned over the summer. He would try to learn a new language or some musical instrument in the summer. He stressed how important it was to always be learning, and that those things somehow made him a better math teacher. I had a hard time wrapping my head around that one. Voluntarily taking a class over the summer or teaching yourself something out of a book or with a video seemed like insanity to a 12-year-old boy. He also asked me what books I read over the summer knowing full well that I was not about to read a book unless I was forced to do so. He was always a teacher even when we weren't in class.

When I got to Mr. Woods classroom there were a bunch of younger students piling into the door. I made my way in to find an unfamiliar face writing some stuff on the board.

"Good morning!"

"Good morning. Where's Mr. Woods?"

"Oh, I haven't met Mr. Woods yet. This is my first day. He must be assigned to a different room. I'm Mrs. Evans. What's your name?"

"I'm Richie. I think you're my math teacher this year."

"That's great! I'm looking forward to having you in class, Richie. It was nice to meet you."

I made my way out past the little kids coming into the room and started down the hall toward my homeroom. I was stopping at each classroom along the way to see if Mr. Woods was around, but we wasn't. I didn't have time to search the whole building, so I went to the front office to ask where his new classroom was. There was a ton of people in line. Mostly it was younger kids with their moms. Some of the very young kids were crying as was pretty typical for the first day of school. Some of the kids were older and held pieces of official looking paper in their hands. I figured they were probably transfers from some other school. I waited impatiently hoping I could get to the front of the line before the bell rang to be in homeroom. It was going to be close. Most of the inquiries were ridiculous. They needed to know which room to report to even though it said it right on the papers you always got over the summer. Some were more important like giving the nurse some medication the kid had to take during the school day. I finally got to the front of the line. Mrs. Cokely was at the front desk every year since I started at St. Ann. She retired at the end of the previous year. There was a Sister at the front desk now. She was new to the school. I didn't recognize her. The name plate on the front desk said, *Sister Helen*.

"Good morning, young man!"

"Good morning. Can you tell which room Mr. Woods is in this year? I went to his usual class, but he wasn't there."

"Oh, Mr. Woods? I haven't yet met Mr. Woods."

She turned toward Mrs. Schilling as she spoke. Mrs. Schilling was basically the glue that kept the whole place running. If something was going on at the school, Mrs. Schilling was part of it. She was there forever and knew everything. She should have made some of whatever they were paying everyone else because she would do her job and a little of everyone else's job. She would know where Mr. Woods' new class was. Mrs. Schilling was typing into a typewriter when Sister Helen turned to her in confusion about Mr. Woods. Mrs. Schilling got up from her desk and looked to see who was asking the question. She gave me one of those looks that adults give kids when they know something that they don't want you to know. I got a bad feeling right away. Something was wrong. Mr. Woods wasn't a teacher at St. Ann's anymore. How could they make Mr. Woods leave? He was the best teacher in the school. I started getting really mad. They keep crappy teachers and make the best ones leave. They were so dumb. This school sucks so bad. If Mr. Woods was gone, I should just go to Wilson. I should just leave right now and tell my parents I want to go to Wilson. We could save money. We really didn't have the money for catholic school anyway. How was I going to deal with math without Mr. Woods around? The bell rang for homeroom, but I wasn't going anywhere. I needed an answer. I needed to know. How could they be so dumb to let Mr. Woods go.

Mrs. Schilling turned and quickly walked over to Mr. Hughes' office and gave a light knock before letting herself in. The parents behind me started moving up to the front desk and asking Sister Helen whatever stupid thing they were there to ask. I got shuffled off to the side of the desk. The crying was getting louder and more annoying. It was taking too long. They were probably in there cooking up some story to tell me, so they didn't have to tell me the truth. I moved over in front of Sister Helen again. I was tired of waiting on the side.

"Do you know what's going on and you just don't want to tell me?"

"No. No, it's not that, son. I promise."

She reached out and touched my hand when she spoke. She seemed really nice, but I was too upset to care. Mrs. Schilling came out of the principal's office closely followed by Mr. Hughes. He came up to the front desk and held the swinging door open.

"C'mon in, Richie."

He tried to say it with an upbeat tone, but I could tell he wasn't upbeat. I walked back into Mr. Hughes' office. There were some other kids already in the room. I recognized most of them as kids that I saw getting extra help from Mr. Woods after school or at lunchtime. Brian was there sitting next to Scott. I knew they would also go to Mr. Woods for extra math help. I sat down in an empty seat next to them. Mrs. Howell was there as well. She was our guidance director. She was always around if there was something not good going on at school. We usually saw her at assemblies before a major event or a field trip. She would lead the session explaining how much trouble we would be in if we even thought about doing something wrong at the event. She would also lead the assemble that would take place after any school event to talk about all the things that we did wrong at the event. She would read off a list of the stuff that went on and let us know that we would never be allowed to have another event like the one we just had if we ever acted like that again. The kids called her "The Face" because she always had this face on like she was really mad and about to give you bad news. It was just her normal face even if she was just walking around in the hall.

"This is bad. We're screwed."

"Chill, Lad. Ya don't know what this about. It's the first day of school. It could be anything."

"No, this is about that fight at the park. This is us getting suspended for fighting."

"Crazy talk, Scott. That was in the summer. You can't get in trouble at school for something you did over the summer. Besides why are all these other kids here? Are they in trouble for fighting at the park? By the way it was hardly a fight. You punched a kid and he went down. Why are Richie and me here? We didn't fight. If anybody was getting in trouble for that, it would just be you, you maniac."

"Oh, okay. Just me then. I gotta take the rap for all of us. Okay. I can handle it."

"Handle what? Richie talk some sense into this muppet."

"This aint about the fight. I wish it was about the fight. It's much worse."

"What could be worse? You're both nuts. The Face is here. You know it's bad news. What else could it be with The Face here??"

"Shut up for a second."

Mr. Hughes and Mrs. Howell were talking quietly in the corner of the room. I wished Brian and Scott would shut up, so I could hear what they were saying. I was sure if I could hear them, I would know what the truth was. I was certain they were probably talking about what lies to tell us. They could never just tell us what was real. We were always too young to know the truth.

"We'll see. If Mr. Hughes talks to us, then it might not be too bad. If it's The Face, we're dead."

Brian and I just looked at each other and shook our heads. The Face stepped forward to address the room.

"Yup, we're dead."

"Good morning, students. I am afraid I have some bad news for you all. I know that you have all received extra help in math from Mr. Woods in past years. Some of you have been his students for many years and developed very special relationships with him."

I whispered to Brian. "I'm done here. Fuck this school."

I stood up from my seat and threw my bookbag over my shoulder.

"Dude. Sit down. What are you doing? You're going to get suspended."

Brian was pulling on my pants trying to get me back into my seat. The Face never skipped a beat. She just kept talking. The rest of the kids were staring at me. I was trying to wrestle Brian's hand off my pant leg.

"Mr. Woods is no longer with us."

Brian let go of my pant leg. I took a step forward on my way toward enrolling at Wilson.

"I am very sad to tell you that Mr. Woods passed away over the summer."

I fell back into my seat. A few of the girls in the room let out audible gasps. Everyone else just sat there in shock. During the time I went to St. Ann's a few teachers had passed away, but not until they had retired from teaching and were gone from the school for a few years. We didn't have any active teachers pass away before.

"Mr. Woods became ill at the end of last year. He didn't share the news with very many people. He didn't want there to be any ceremonies or any fuss made on his behalf."

She went on a bit about Mr. Woods, but I couldn't hear any of it. I couldn't understand why he didn't tell me he was sick. We were friends, weren't we? He wasn't just my teacher. Did he not think of me as his friend? These other kids couldn't have known him like I did. They just needed to know how they will get help for math now that Mr. Woods was gone. I was becoming resentful that they were in the room. I wasn't there about tutoring. They could have had a separate meeting. I was there because my friend died. I was trying not to cry. Only the girls were crying.

Mrs. Howell and Mr. Hughes stepped out of the room. They said we could stay as long as we felt like we needed to before returning to class. Some of the kids left soon after. Others started filing out a few minutes later.   Brian was the first of us to leave. We never said a word. Once it got down to only Scott and I in the room, Mr. Hughes walked back in and closed the door. He grabbed a chair and moved it over in front of where Scott and I were sitting.

"I'm sorry, boys. Bob...Mr. Woods was a very private man. Only his family and a few of his friends knew about his illness. He didn't want anyone to do anything special for him. It's just how he was."

Bob?. I didn't realize until that moment that Mr. Hughes knew Mr. Woods as more than one of the teachers he supervised. I really had never thought of teachers as people with lives outside of the school. Mr. Hughes noticed that I realized he had called Mr. Woods 'Bob'.

"We were friends since elementary school. We were roommates in college."

He showed us a picture he had in his wallet of the two during their college years. It was odd and kind of funny seeing them both so much younger. He had a picture of them at a wedding. He said they were each other's best man. He handed each of us a small envelope. They had our names on the front. I recognized Mr. Wood's writing. That's when I had to try the hardest to not cry.

"He wanted you to have these. You can read them here if you want."

He turned and left the room and closed the door behind him. Only then did I realize that Scott was one of the people Mr. Woods was close with. I was surprised that he was close enough with him that he left Scott a note. I turned toward Scott and he must have seen that I was confused by his presence.

"He was the only one who could help me with math. Mrs. Biggs sucks. I wouldn't even know how to add if it wasn't for Mr. Woods. I'm so screwed now. But it wasn't just math, ya know. I would talk with him about everything. He was trying to help me with my anger issues. Yeah, I know I got anger issues. I don't want to be a jerk, Richie. It just happens sometimes. He's probably so disappointed that I punched that kid."

I was actually connecting with Scott. He was saying a lot of the things that I had felt about Mr. Woods and math, and how Mr. Woods was more than just one of my teachers. I never felt that way before. Usually I couldn't understand why Scott was saying the things he would say. That day it was like he was speaking all the things that were in my head. He had tears in his eyes as he tore open his note and started reading. He was smiling at one point and let out a little laugh at another. Then he got sad and teared up again. He tried folding up the note and stuffing it back into the envelope. He was getting frustrated because he wasn't folding it right, and it wouldn't go back in the right way. I reached out to take the note. He drew it back from me.

"I'm not trying to read it. I can get it back in for you."

He handed me the note and the open envelope. I folded it up and slipped it back inside.

"Thanks! You gonna read yours?"

"Not yet. I think I'll wait until I get home."

"OK. I'll see you in class."

Scott stood up to leave. I sat there looking at the envelope. It felt good to be one of the few people Mr. Woods wrote a note to before he died. I felt special. He always made me feel good and was doing it now even though he was gone. Mr. Hughes came back into his office.

"You okay?"

"Yeah. No."

"I know what you mean." He noticed the unopen letter in my hand.

"Gonna wait until later? Ok. You know I used to teach math. I can help if you need it. Just let me know."

"Thanks."

I got up and went to class. The rest of the day was as weird as a day of school could be. It was good that it was mostly going over rules and grading and getting new books and supplies, rather than any real lessons. I wouldn't have learned a thing that day. It was like I was on autopilot. It looked the same for Scott from what I could tell. I caught him daydreaming and staring out the window at times. It was the first time I felt a real connection to Scott. I didn't think he had any emotions other than anger before that day. That was stupid of me. He never shared what was in his letter, and he never asked me what was in mine. We got along better after that day, not that we were ever as close as me and Terry. It was much better though.

I was dreading getting home and having my parents ask me how my day went. It went lousy. It was the worst day ever. They wouldn't want to hear that. They would be excited about the first day of school and would want to hear how great it was. It always seemed like a bother to talk about my day when I was that age. It seemed like an invasion, like my parents were snooping on me to see if I did something wrong. I never really explained much about how my day went, I mostly gave them my standard '*it was fine*'. When I got home from the bus stop that day, my mom was sitting on the steps waiting. It only took one look for me to know that she already knew. Someone from the school must have called her. She never asked how my day went. She just hugged me.

"Why didn't he tell me?"

"Sounds like he didn't tell very many people, Richie. It wasn't just you. It was just his way. It doesn't mean he wasn't your friend."

"He left me a note."

"Well, see. I'm sure he only wrote to those people who were special to him."

"Do you want to read it?"

"That's your letter from your friend. I will read it with you, or you can read it in private. Whatever you want."

I was surprised by that answer. I thought she would want to read it. I always thought that in her mind I didn't have anything that was private. I stared at the note for a second before putting it back in my bag unopened. I went to my room and got changed to go outside. My mom said she would order pizza for dinner. That was my favorite food. We always got pizza any time I was upset about anything and my parents wanted to cheer me up.

I struggled through some games at the school with the crew that day. It was a typical day for everyone other than Scott and me. Scott was subdued. He was chill the whole time and never gave any of us a hard time about anything. At one point he said, "Your best is good enough" after someone botched something. It was odd to hear, not just because us doing our best had never been good enough for Scott before. That was something Mr. Woods would always say to me. It was like I got an insight into what Mr. Woods wrote Scott in his note. Scott was different after that day. He was still hard on us and drove us to play better, but he wasn't like before. He was more about encouragement than he was before that. He still had his moments, but it was a lot easier to be around him. It occurred to me that if Mr. Woods accomplished nothing else with his life, helping Scott be a better person seemed like a big enough accomplishment for a lifetime.

"You think your mom will let me stay over tonight. My mom got me Asteroids. I can bring it over."

"Awesome! Let's go ask."

My mom was going to be cool with just about anything I wanted after that first day of school. Usually school nights were not sleep over nights, but that night was different. I went with Terry over to his house to get his stuff. I was excited about playing Asteroids all night. That was one of our favorite games to play when we went to the arcade. It was cool to be able to play it whenever we wanted right at home. I loved video games because I could actually be competitive with Terry. I was nowhere near his level at anything else. Plus, with Terry over for the night, I didn't have to face reading the letter from Mr. Woods.

"Uncle John is already on his way over to stay with you tonight. He's gonna be disappointed. You sure you don't want to have Richie stay here tonight. I bet your uncle would like to try Asteroids too."

"Hey, that would be cool. We could all..."

"No. We already talked to Richie's mom about it. I'm gonna stay there."

Terry quickly grabbed his stuff and we took off for my house. I had a good time that night even though I kept stealing glances to where Mr. Wood's note seemed to be burning a hole through the bottom of my school bag. We ate pizza and stayed up too late like always, but it was a pleasant distraction from the worst day ever.

Letters

Oh, okay. This is just great. Now there's letters in the math problems? What the hell?? I was having enough trouble when it was just numbers; now we got letters in the math problems. Whose idea was this?? I bet Mrs. Biggs invented this math just to torture us. Letters?!? Really. This has to be a joke. Are we on Candid Camera or something?

I was losing my mind over pre-Algebra. Mrs. Evans was a pretty good teacher, and if I could have managed my anger over there being letters in math class, I might have understood better. Nobody could replace Mr. Woods, but she wasn't bad. I looked around and it appeared I wasn't the only one having issues. Some of the faces were comical to be honest. It was nice to know I wasn't the only one in the class struggling to deal with the letter 'x' finding its way into our math lives.

"Only Americans would put letters in the math problems."

"They don't do math like this in Ireland?"

"Are you kidding? I haven't understood a thing come out of her gob in thirty minutes. If they did this in Ireland, kids would be on the lash most afternoons."

I wasn't sure exactly what Brian said, but I could tell it wasn't good. Just past where Brian was introducing me to new Irish sayings for how bad American math was, I caught a glimpse of Scott. His mouth was stuck in the open position, and it looked like he was about to cry. Brian and I got a kick out of it until he noticed we were looking at him.

"It's not funny. What the hell is this?? There's letters now?!"

"Don't get upset. We can go see Mr. Hughes. He said he would help if we need it."

I was trying to be reassuring, but I wasn't truly sure if Mr. Hughes could help us. I didn't know if his offer for help was just one of those things adults would say but didn't really mean. I also didn't know if he had any time for us. He was the principal. He probably needed to do principal things after school. He probably didn't have any time to be translating letter math to us.

"Every day I miss Mr. Woods more."

"You know they were talking about this new thing called 'block calendar' or something like that. It means you spend way more time in each class. Like two hours in every class."

"What? How would that work? We'd be in class until like ten o'clock at night."

"Just imagine two hours of this stuff."

"I think I'm just going to slam my head into my desk until I pass out."

The bell rang just as we were trying to figure out if Scott was serious about the head slamming thing.

"Oh, sweet music of the Lord."

The bell made everything feel better. We forgot about math almost instantly and were giving each other *wet willies* as we headed into the hall. I was doing fine in my other classes. Math was always the main concern. At 2:30 Brian, Scott, and I made our way into the main office. Mr. Hughes wasn't there, so Sister Helen had us to sit in the chairs near the front desk and wait for him. When he got to the office, Mr. Hughes' tie was twisted and hanging off to the side, and he had a pained look on his face as was typical by the afternoon. He saw the three of us sitting there. I think he assumed we were there because we did something wrong.

"What do we have here, Sister Helen?"

"These young men said that you offered to help them with their math work. They were hoping you had some time this afternoon."

Mr. Hughes face immediately brightened. The hunch he would walk around with, the one that got more curved and pronounced as the school day progressed, disappeared. He straightened up and it seemed like he was half a foot taller than he was when he walked into the office.

"Oh, okay. Sure. Sure. C'mon in."

He held the swinging door open for us.

"Let's go in my office."

"There's letters in the problems now. Letters! Have you heard about this?"

It's alright, Scott. We'll figure it out."

He smiled at Sister Helen. I don't know if I had seen Mr. Hughes smile before that. It turned out that he wasn't just saying he would help us with math. He made time for us that day and whenever we asked. He was great at teaching math. He had the same way of teaching as Mr. Woods. He could take anything and make it seem so simple just like Mr. Woods did. We were crushing it after a few sessions with Mr. Hughes. I got a 97 on the first test. I was thrilled. I hadn't seen a grade that high in math in forever. I wished that I could tell Mr. Woods. He always wanted me to shoot for an A in math, but the truth was that I really wasn't hoping for much more than a C, even with extra help. If I didn't make a silly mistake on one problem, I would have gotten 100.

Scott got 100 on that first test. I can still see his face when Mrs. Evans handed him his paper back. He was glowing. He never got grades like that before in math. It was cool to watch him staring at his test. He was so proud. He was never anything but angry in math class before that. Mr. Hughes changed the way we looked at a math problem. He turned into a game. It was almost fun. Almost. I think what I appreciated most about the extra time Mr. Woods and Mr. Hughes spent with us is that they relieved the stress I felt about math. I remember how I would start feeling anxious in the class before math. It would really ramp up as I went to my locker and started walking toward the classroom. They changed that. There was always so much stress to being in middle school. Not just stress about classwork, but stress about life. Mr. Woods was able to reduce the stress, and after working with Mr. Hughes for a while it got even better. I don't think I ever completely lost that feeling of dread as the time for math class approached, but I was much less anxious.

Walking home was the price of staying after school for help with math. It was worth it. School wasn't that far from my house. I lived just over the line that they used to determine whether you got bussing or not. Glen Firth lived around the block from us. He was just inside the line where you didn't qualify for bussing. Glen was known for rarely arriving at school with a clean uniform on. He would ride his bike to school if it wasn't raining too hard or too cold outside. On some days our bus would pass him on the way to school. Those weren't good mornings for Glen. If we passed anyone on the way to school, it usually meant that poor kid got pelted with whatever the kids on the bus could find to throw out the window. Glen started more than a few days of school with some kind of food on his uniform or red marks on his face where a rubber ball or something else hit him. I kinda understood the non-food items. I didn't get why anyone would throw their snack out the window. It seemed like a waste. I always wanted to eat my snack if I had one. My mom wouldn't always put a snack in my lunch. She thought it should be a treat, rather than an everyday thing. Glen got smart after a while and started walking to our bus stop in the morning. Mr. Reilly didn't care that he wasn't authorized for busing. Problem solved. It was a lot safer and Glen was a lot happier...and cleaner when he got to school.

The walk home was fine if the weather was good. If it was cold, it was a problem. There's something about the genetic makeup of young American males that make them resist wearing proper outerwear in cold weather. I was no different. Huge coats are seen as uncool for some odd reason. We would much rather have on a light jacket that is not nearly appropriate for the conditions than to maintain a comfortable body temperature under a massive and uncool winter coat. You can observe this behavior in the male of the species across the nation. It wasn't just our town or our generation. This is everywhere, and it continues even today. If you are out on a cold day near the time the kids in your town are heading to bus stops or walking to school, you will find several boys shivering their asses off under some flimsy windbreaker, if they are wearing any jacket at all. There is a lightly worn perfectly stylish coat in the closet of just about every boy between the ages of 11 and 18. The garment will hang there mostly unused until it is either passed down to a younger male sibling, in which case the change simply means hanging it in a different closet of the home, or it is donated to charity or thrown away. Shivering is cool. Hypothermia is cool. Coats are not cool.

I had a few strategic shortcuts I could use to shorten the walk home. I would always cut down the alley behind the bank even though it said, 'No Trespassing'. Nobody really cared about a school kid walking by there. I could hop the fence at the McDonald's house. They were an older couple who never noticed kids cutting through their yard. That would bring me out by Beacon Street. All in all, walking home took only a few minutes more than riding the bus home when you factor in the shortcuts I would take and all the stops the bus would make.

As I got through the McDonald's yard, I started thinking about the unopened note from Mr. Woods. It was still at the bottom of my book bag. I kept finding reasons not to read it. I was searching for a good excuse again not to take it out right then and there and read it as I walked home. Despite trying very hard, I couldn't invent a good reason not to open it. I dug it out from under my books and stared at my name written across the front of the envelope. It still does something to me even today to see my name in Mr. Woods' handwriting on that envelope. I carefully ran my finger under the seal and flipped the top open. I took it out of the envelope and started to unfold it.

"Richie!"

I forgot that Jimmy lived on Beacon Street. I hurriedly folded the note and inserted it back in my book bag. Jimmy was in his garage with his little sister. He had her bike upside down in some vice grips that were attached to a big work bench and was working on something. His garage was ultra-organized. There was a pegboard with more tools and stuff on it than even Mr. Wilbur had at school. There were big cabinets for tools and the workbench with the vice grips had neatly organized drawers and stuff all around. Nothing was out of place in there. I remember our garage looking like we purposely just threw things everywhere. It was hard to even walk to the back of our garage without falling over stuff. Annie, Jimmy's little sister was next to him watching him work. I think she was about five or six at the time. Her bike, Like Jimmy's, was a collection of parts from multiple bikes. The seat said *Strawberry Shortcake*. It had a bunch of pictures of strawberries on it. It was white and pink and red. There was a metal cover over where the chain was. It was yellow and said *Sweet Miss*. There was a little white and red basket attached in front of the handlebars. Annie would always have a doll in that basket when she was riding. There was a sign over the basket attached to the handlebars that said *Sweet Thunder* with a number 2.

"You like my bike, Richie?"

"I like it a lot. It's really cool."

"Jimmy's putting butterflies on my bike. It's going to be more cooler."

"Awesome!"

Jimmy was attaching these butterfly clips to the spokes on the back wheel. From inside the house I heard Jimmy's dad start yelling. Then I could hear his mom yelling and there was some loud banging.

"Jimmy."

Annie started nervously jumping up and down. Jimmy immediately stopped what he was doing and put down the butterfly clip he had in his hand. He picked up his sister and sat her in a little chair along the side of the garage. The chair was a perfect size for her, and there were a bunch of little girl toys and dolls arranged perfectly on either side. In front of the chair was a box with coloring books, crayons, and old Barbie dolls. His sister was still kind of jumping up and down rapidly in her seat. Jimmy reached up on the shelf over the chair and took down a Walkman. It was a lot like the one he would wear at the bus stop each day. It was taped together with some duct tape and the color of the unit was different than the color of the headphones.

He quickly set the unit on a box next to the chair and placed the headphones over his sister's head. She settled down as the music started. He handed her one of the coloring books. She started coloring and the nervousness disappeared. Jimmy stepped back and took a look at her to see if she was okay. His dad was still yelling inside the house. I didn't hear his mom yelling any more, but there was still a ton of loud noises and banging. Jimmy turned and looked at me. He was clearly embarrassed. I wished that I never walked into that garage. I should have just waved and kept going. I could have been reading the note from Mr. Woods on the way home and not seen any of this.

"I should go."

"I could use some help with this one." Jimmy pointed at his bike.

"Ok."

Jimmy never needed any help from anyone when working on a bike. Jimmy grabbed his Walkman from the side of the workbench. He set it beside me and held out the headphones. The yelling in the house continued.

"I got some cool tunes. You could listen as we work."

I hated the look on his face. His eyes were swelling with tears. He was ashamed. I wanted to tell him it was okay. I didn't know how. I knew why he wanted me to listen to the music. I wasn't about to refuse.

"Ok. Cool."

We were both poorly pretending that everything was alright. He turned on the music and took his sister's bike out the vice grips. He set it down next to where she was sitting. She jumped up and gave him a hug. She knelt down next to the bike and was running her hands over the butterfly clips. Jimmy grabbed his bike and set it in the vice grips. I was stunned at how easily he flipped it over and secured it into position. I had a hard time moving my bike around when it was upright and on its wheels. He started working. He would gesture where he wanted me to hold something or hand him a different tool. I wasn't sure what he was doing or even if anything was broken. It all seemed fine to me. The music was loud but not loud enough to completely cover up the sounds from inside the house. I could see him flinch a little each time there was a loud noise from the house. Every so often he would wipe away a tear. I would pretend not to notice.

Born down in a dead man's town
The first kick I took was when I hit the ground
You end up like a dog that's been beat too much
'Til you spend half your life just coverin' up

I dropped a screwdriver and it rolled under the workbench. I got down on my knees to find it. Jimmy's dad came out the house. He slammed the door to the house so hard that some of the toys fell off the shelf around Jimmy's sister. I heard the bang through the music. I could feel it too. I could see Jimmy's dad's work boots from under the workbench. His dad took a few steps toward where we were working on the bike. I stood up once I got the screwdriver. Jimmy's dad was surprised to see me. I don't think he knew I was there until that moment. He tried to seem calm, but it wasn't working.

"Hi Richie."

"Hi, Mr. Sullivan."

"I gotta go to work. Make sure all the tools are put back when you're done."

Mr. Sullivan started walking out of the garage. He walked right by Annie but never said goodbye. He got in his car and drove off. Jimmy and Annie were clearly relieved once he left. Jimmy walked over to his sister and removed the headphones. He helped her wheel her bike out of the garage. We stood in the front of his house and watched as she rode back and forth up to the corner and back. I think she had only learned to ride without training wheels a few days before.

"I'm doing good, right Jimmy."

"You're doing great, Annie."

"Just to the corner then I turn around."

"That's right."

I was trying to find something to talk about to fill the uncomfortable silence while we watched Annie pedal away. I should have just said something about school. I could have talked about the new math teacher. I could have talked about something that happened when we were playing baseball the day before. There was a ton of things I could have said, but my head was filled with nothing but the thought of Jimmy in that garage hiding his little sister from the nightmare unfolding in their house. It was like the whole scene hit the reset button on my brain. I was waiting for anything to come into my head, so I could make things easier for both of us. I was waiting and waiting, but nothing happened. I waited too long.

"He's not so bad most of the time."

"Oh, sure. I know."

"He's cool most of the time. He just gets real mad once in a while."

"Yeah, my dad too. He gets really angry sometimes. Everyone's dad does."

We watched Annie turn the corner and start back toward us.

"Alright. I gotta get home or my parents are going to wonder where I am."

"Ok. Thanks for helping me today."

"I hardly did anything – just holding some stuff. You did all the hard stuff."

"No. You were a big help today. Thank you, Richie." He was making a point to look me in the eye when he said thanks. He reached out to shake my hand.

"Sure yeah...anytime."

Jimmy helped Annie off her bike and into the garage. He started replacing the tools into different spots on the pegboard and into different draws around the garage. He gave me a wave as he grabbed the rope to pull the garage door down. I gave him a wave and started toward home. I was disappointed in myself. I should have said something. How could I not find something to say? I should have been able to come up with something, anything to say so he didn't feel like he had to explain about his dad. I was hoping to have a chance to talk to him that night at the school. I could make up for being a zero at his house. Terry and I rode over to the school together after dinner. Everyone was there that night. Everyone except Jimmy.

"Where's Sullivan? He was in school today."

"He's probably building a car for when he turns 17."

"You seen him, Richie?"

"I saw him at school. I don't know where he is now."

Nobody gave my answer a second thought. Nobody that is except Terry. While the other kids accepted my answer outright, Terry gave me a look. It was nothing anyone else would have noticed, but I caught it. It was a look he would give me when he knew there was something off. He always seemed to have a way of knowing when I wasn't coming clean about something. He didn't call me on it – not in front of the rest of the crew. We all went about our usual stuff that night, just without Jimmy. On the way home, after I slowed down to see if Kelly was in the hedges at the Mercer's place, he asked me about it.

"You know something about Jimmy that you didn't tell everyone?"

"You can't tell anybody, promise?"

"Yeah. Promise. What's the deal?"

"I think Jimmy's dad beat up his mom today."

"How do you know?"

I told him the whole story even the part where I felt like a failure for not saying more.

"Oh, that's what it is."

"That's what what is?"

"I've seen the cops over there a few times."

"The cops?"

"Yeah, it's happened a couple times this summer. I can kinda see Jimmy's place from my bedroom window. The cops came to his house a couple times this summer. They never put anybody in the car though, so I didn't know what it was about, and I wasn't going to ask him."

"Should we do something?"

"Like what? What can we do?"

"I don't know. Tell the police."

"I think it's too late. Jimmy didn't say he was going to call the police?"

"No. He just said his dad's cool most of the time. That he gets mad sometimes."

"Yeah, he must get really mad. I think Jimmy would be upset if you told the cops."

"So, we can't do anything?"

"I don't think so. Nobody can help anybody."

I was frustrated with that answer. I wanted there to be something we could do. Terry just turned away and rode into his driveway after he said it. I wanted to argue with him. It didn't seem right that we couldn't help anyone. I was mad that he said that and then just left before I could argue with him. I wanted to help. It was another reminder that when I had a chance earlier that day, I didn't do anything. I just left Jimmy hanging there - ashamed and feeling like he needed to tell me some story to make it right.

When I got to my room, I was thinking about the note again. If I had just kept walking and reading, that day might have went better. I was trying to figure out if I would feel better after reading the note. Maybe it would cheer me up. I was thinking Mr. Woods would have some way of making me feel better about everything and about him being gone. I wanted to be sure it would be a good thing. I didn't want any more to feel lousy about. I know just seeing it made me sad, but I was thinking if I opened it quickly and started reading, there would be good things inside. I was wishing Mr. Woods was still alive, so I could tell him about Jimmy. He would tell me what I could do to help. He would have the answer.

"Hey there, Champ."

"Hi, Dad."

"How was your day?"

"It was fine."

"Another fine day, huh? You have a lot of those. Ok. You got homework? I'll let you get to it."

He started walking out.

"Dad."

I could see he was surprised and pleased that I had something more to say. I would typically try to find the quickest way to end a conversation with my parents, rather than extend one.

"Do you think reading Mr. Woods' note will make me feel good or bad?"

"You haven't read it yet, huh?"

"Not yet. I don't want to read it if it's going to make me feel bad."

"Well, I don't think there's a guarantee that it won't make you feel bad."

"Have you ever gotten a note like that."

"No, not quite like that one."

"So, you don't know?"

He sat down next to me on the floor next to my bed.

"Nope, I don't know for sure. I don't think there's a way to know what a letter will make you feel until you read it. But what I think is that a letter like that from someone you cared about who's not here anymore, will probably make you feel good and bad."

"How can someone feel good and bad at the same time?"

"I think that Mr. Woods was a special guy, and you were friends. So, that means his thoughts and what he wrote you before he died are going to make you feel good. But once you read it, it will be sad because it's the last time you get to kinda hear his voice in your head, and it's the last experience you'll have of him. So, that part will be sad."

He must have seen the confusion on my face. I didn't know how happy and sad could mix inside me at the same time.

"It will make more sense as time goes by, Champ."

He smiled at me as he got up. He made a loud exaggerated noise as dads always do when they get up off the floor. He took a look at the closed door; then he put his finger to his lips to signal me to be quiet. He carefully and slowly stepped to the door and then opened it really fast. My mom was standing there in the doorway. She pretended she was just walking by, but he caught her big time.

"Oh, hey. What are you guys talking about?"

"We were talking about how Cancer sucks."

"Hey! C'mon. I don't want Richie talking like that."

"Good night, Champ!"

He walked out and closed the door behind him. I sat around for a few minutes thinking about what my dad said. After a while I opened my book bag and took out my spelling book. There was a test the next day. I needed to study.

Courage

"You sure she goes to Wilson?"

"Well, she's not at our school. Where else can she go?"

"I don't know. There's no new girls this year. Not any named Kelly."

"How many eighth-grade classes are there?"

"There's three. I've seen all the kids though. I know everybody. Nobody new named Kelly. We got a Kelly Smith, but she's not new, and she's not super-hot. If there was a new super-hot girl, I would have definitely noticed her by now."

Tommy was my only connection at Wilson. I figured he would know if Kelly was going to school there. She had to be. How can you not go to school? I guess she could be at All Saints. All Saints was an all-girl school. All Saints was super expensive though. Nobody from our town went to All Saints. I didn't know anyone who went there who I could ask either. Maybe she was at All Saints. She said that she was from California, and I was pretty sure everyone from California was rich, so maybe she could afford it.

"That's where all the movie stars live. They are all rich, so she's probably rich too."

"Makes sense that she would be at All Saints being rich from California."

"Maybe Todd can hide out in the girl's bathroom at All Saints and let us know if she goes to school there."

"Oh, hilarious."

"Are you sure she really exists, Richie? Maybe you dreamed her. It doesn't look like anybody lives in the Cody house."

"I didn't dream her. I've seen her. Terry has seen her too. She's real and she lives there with her dad."

"How does a kid, even a girl, stay in the house all summer? That's torture."

"I think she's locked away in Richie's mind."

"I think she might be locked away in Richie's pants. She lives there with his hand."

"Why don't you just knock on the door and ask if she can come outside."

"All this time and you never just knocked on the door and asked her to come outside?"

'No, her dad looks like a murderer. He's a scary dude. I'm not knocking on the door."

I was sorry I asked Tommy about Kelly, but I was getting desperate. I hadn't seen Kelly in a couple of weeks and before that was the time that I went over there with my Mom to deliver the cake. Two sightings in about four months – she was like Haley's comet. It would have been worth the verbal abuse if Tommy had seen her at school. The fact that he hadn't just made Kelly even more of a mystery. Plus, now the whole crew knew, and I had to get an earful of nonsense.

"Can we just play now?"

"I think we should see if the fantasy girl wants to play, we could use another player anyway since Raji isn't here."

"She's a girl. We don't even know if she can catch."

"I think we can safely assume she is a better baseball player than you, Richie. So, we could definitely use her."

"Assume this."

"Yeah, let's go see Richie's dream girl."

"She's not my dream girl."

She was every bit my dream girl.

"Yeah, what's her dad going to do, murder all of us?"

"I don't think it's a good idea."

"I think it's a great idea."

The whole crew started walking toward their bikes. I was not nearly as enthusiastic about the plan as everyone else was.

"I think we should just play. Let's just play."

"C'mon, Richie. You're coming. We are going to see this girl and her scary dad."

I followed a few steps behind the bunch as they got on their bikes.

"Just get on your bike. Let's go, Guys."

I peddled slowly behind the group. I wasn't going to be in the front in case her dad exploded out of the house with a machete. I also didn't want Kelly to think having the whole crew show up at her door was a plan that I endorsed in any way. I wasn't sure she would fit in with us. She was rich girl from California. She might be used to guys like the ones from the next town over. She might be used to guys with money and great houses and cool stuff. I was deeply regretting ever mentioning her to anyone other than Terry. She probably would forget about me the moment she saw Scott or Terry or Billy. They were bigger and way better looking than me. She would surely be done with me if she did come out to play with us. She would see how uncoordinated I was, and I would have no chance. This was definitely a lousy idea. I was so stupid to say anything.

It was a short ride to the house. As we got closer, the pace slowed dramatically. The house looked dark and uninhabited like it always did. It seemed like the bicycles were now racing in reverse, trying to slow down enough so not to be first to the front of the house. It was hard to ride a bike that slowly without falling off. All the courage we saw on display back at the school was disappearing quickly. It was a six-way tie for first as everyone but me reached the curb in front of the house. I stopped directly across the street. Terry rode up next to me.

"This should be hilarious. None of them will have the nuts to knock."

I was hoping Terry was right. It would be great to see Kelly, but I still wanted to keep her for my own. In my head she was kinda my girlfriend. I didn't want her to meet anyone else. I wanted to be the only boy she knew. As soon as she met the other guys, she would surely lose interest in me. I wanted to see her, but at the same time I didn't. I wished there was some way to keep her for myself. I was so sorry I opened my big mouth.

"Ok, Scott. Knock on the door."

"You knock."

"This was your idea. Go knock.'

Oh, now you're not going to knock."

"I didn't say I would knock. I just said we should knock. WE."

"All that tough talk before, and now you're afraid to knock."

"You guys were talking tough too. Why don't one of you knock."

"Pussy."

"You're a pussy. Go knock, O'Grady."

"Talkin' like the chancer at the field now we see it's all shite. I'll go, but you're not gonna bunk off."

Scott just stared at Brian with a blank look on his face.

"You're coming with me, Big Man."

"Fine. Let's do it."

Scott and Brian got off their bikes and stood at the head the walkway to the house. Neither wanted to be an inch in front of the other as they went to the door. They stepped in time like synchronized swimmers staring at each other and occasionally the front door. It was like a weird Olympic event where they graded you on cowardice and how slow you could walk. At the rate they were moving, they would reach the house in about a week.

"Oh, c'mon. It's gonna be dark soon."

"Are you gonna hold hands?"

"I don't see you wusses up here. "

Scott was looking back at the rest of the crew, but he caught sight of someone back at the school.

"Is that her?"

There was a girl standing there where we usually met each day. We could only make out her silhouette. She looked to have her arms folded as she stood alongside her bike staring down the street at us. She was a dark figure against the red sky and the setting sun. I couldn't be sure, but I didn't think it was Kelly.

"Is that Kelly?"

"I don't know. I can't tell for sure. I don't think so."

Brian and Scott were only too happy to reverse the three painfully slow steps they took back to their bikes. The whole crew was just fine going back to the field without ever having knocked on the door to Kelly's house. I was half relieved and half disappointed. I wanted to see Kelly, but this wasn't how I wanted it. The guys got started on their way back to the field and were at top speed in a few seconds. I lagged behind as I did on the way there. I turned my bike around and took a last look at the house. It was a typical night – there were no signs of life. I headed back to the field.

The guys had rode back and now stood over their bikes in our traditional bike formation. We were about ten feet from the 'stranger' who stood with her arms folded staring back at us.

"Marie."

"What were you dorks doing over there?"

"We wanted to meet Richie's girlfriend."

"You have a girlfriend, Richie."

"No, don't listen to them."

"Are we going to play or are you guys going to stare at me all night?"

Everyone jumped off their bikes. I think we were all excited about having Marie back, but at least a small part of the excitement was that she rescued us from knocking on Kelly's door. Everyone was high-fiving and fist-bumping Marie. Todd sheepishly stepped over to Marie.

"Hi, Marie."

"Hi, Todd."

Todd extended his fist, not sure if he was going to be left hanging. Marie gave him a smile and bumped his fist. Scott grabbed a bat and a ball and headed toward the plate to hit some out to us. Marie ran out to shortstop. Tommy had been playing shortstop – poorly – since Marie stopped coming around earlier that summer. He was not nearly the fielder Marie was.

"Can I play short?"

'I'm our shortstop now."

"Yo. Tommy. Left field."

Tommy didn't argue. He knew he wasn't the player that Marie was. He touched gloves with Marie and sprinted out to left. Marie took her usual spot. It was great having Marie back with us. It made everyone forget about Kelly and giving me a hard time about her. It was either they forgot, or they were content not to have to knock on her door. I was content to not be taking any more abuse. I was also thrilled to have Kelly to myself again in whatever weird way that I thought of her as my own.

Scott ripped a grounder out to Marie at shortstop. She ate it up and sent a rocket over to Billy at first base. She was even smoother with the glove and stronger on her throws than we remembered her.

"Yeah, Marie!"

"Marie's back."

Marie was back, and Kelly was off everyone's mind for now. Well, she was off *almost* everyone's mind.

We played late that night. Except for Todd, we were all okay with getting in a little trouble for being late. Todd had to race home at the usual time. It was exciting to have the full crew back, so we just didn't want to stop playing. Marie was in full beast mode too. I think playing with those guys from the next town raised her game. We would have never admitted it back then, but they were better if you compared the full teams. Terry, Scott, and Billy were just as good if not better than anyone they had, but the rest of us weren't very good. They had no weaknesses. Their worst kid was still good. Just playing for a few weeks with players like that made Marie a better player.

When I got back to my room, I was struggling again to find a plausible rationale for not reading Mr. Wood's note. It was getting harder and harder to fool myself into thinking there was a valid reason to leave it for another day. I was half hoping my parents would walk into my room and want to talk about something just so I could put off opening the note a little longer. It never happened. I had no interruptions and no schoolwork to worry about for the next day. I had nothing left that I could use to validate leaving it there it my bag unopened. I started thinking that Mr. Woods might be disappointed that I hadn't read the note yet. Maybe he would be let down that I didn't have the guts to open it yet. I couldn't live with that thought. It was time.

The envelope with my name on it was just as hard to read as that day when Mr. Hughes handed it to me on the first day of school. I was feeling special again that I was one of the few people who Mr. Woods wrote to before he died. I think now of how he thought to use some of little time he had left for me. I don't think I realized how just significant that was at the time. He knew that he was near death, and he chose to use some of the hours he had left on me. I think now about who I might spend my time on if faced with a similar situation.

Richie,

I hope that you are not disappointed that I didn't tell you that I was sick. It's not a reflection of how I feel about you. You are a special young man and one of my closest friends. I don't think of you as just a student. I hope that is something that was clear from our time together. Our relationship is bigger than math. Our relationship is bigger even than my death. I firmly believe that, and I hope that you do as well. That belief is what is keeps me going now.

I don't want you to be sad. I don't want anyone to be sad. I know that is easier said than done. I can't tell that I am not sad about dying. I don't want to die. I can't tell you that there aren't times when I feel enormous grief and sadness that my time here is coming to an end. I have a million things I wanted to do and so many people with whom I wanted to do them. I love being alive. I am sad that my life is ending, but that sadness is tempered by the joys I have experienced. My time in the classroom, my travels and the experiences I have had, and my relationships with special people like you, Richie, help me to deal with the sadness of my life's end.

I think of our conversations as one of those great experiences. Know that all I tried to do was to help you understand that the answers are within you. You are smarter, more gifted, and stronger than you think. Once you embrace those truths, you will achieve great things. The way you see yourself and what you are capable of is your only limitation, Richie. One of greatest sources of sadness for me is knowing that I will not get to accompany you on your journey. I am so excited for you. Your life will be full of great things. I know this as sure as I know anything about this world.

I hope that you have good feelings when you look back at the time we got to spend together. I certainly do. I remember all the laughs we had. I hope that your life is full of laughter. I think we will laugh again together somewhere down the line.

"The mark of the immature man is that he wants to die nobly for a cause, while the mark of the mature man is that he wants to live humbly for one."

Goodbye for now.

Your friend.

Bob

I understood as soon as the letter ended what my Dad said about it making me feel happy and sad at the same time. I wished there were more pages to read. I wished there were other notes waiting for me to open them. I heard Bob's voice in my head like my Dad said I would. That was special. It still is special to this day. I can still hear his voice in my mind when I read it. It helps me to stay connected to him. I folded the note and placed it back in the envelope. I wished that I had the chance to write Bob a note before he died. I wished that he could have explained the quote to me since I didn't understand it fully at the time. There have been a great many times that I wished here were around to explain things. I realized that I needed to stop feeling that way. He made a point in his note to tell me that. It was just so hard to do.

Rain

It was rainy the next day. It was a bummer because Marie was back, and I think we were all excited to have the whole day to play together again. Things just didn't feel right when Marie left, and they definitely didn't feel right with her playing against us. It was the kind of rainy day I hated. It was raining on and off. It didn't rain really hard or for very long. It was light rain and it would start and stop every fifteen minutes or so. If it was going to be a rainy day, I wanted it to just rain hard all the time. The sporadic rain was aggravating. It was just rainy enough that day to be frustrating. It was wet enough to stop you from doing the things you wanted to do outside, but it gave you false hope that it might stop, and you eventually could go out and play. I hated it when we were stuck somewhere in between.

I didn't mind if it rained during the school day in September. When you're stuck at school, who cares what the weather is like. It was still hot in September, not hot like May and June, but still it was hot. The rain kept the school building cool. We didn't have air conditioning. Whatever the building was made of, it seemed to trap heat inside. It was somehow cooler outside in the sun. It was hard to concentrate on schoolwork on a hot day. All you could think about was how hot you were. We would sweat sometimes just sitting calmly at our desks if it were hot enough outside. For a twelve-year-old boy, wearing a shirt and tie anywhere isn't fun. Wearing a shirt and tie in a hot classroom really isn't any fun. I'm pretty sure the term 'business casual' was invented by a guy who went to Catholic school.

I think our teachers liked it when it rained. The rain calmed us down a bit. The grey skies and the rhythm of the rain does something to kids. When it was quiet, we could hear the rain on the roof. The sound was very soft though, so the class needed to be very quiet to hear it. It wasn't often that one of our classrooms would be quiet enough to hear the rain. If the class did reach a point where it was quiet enough, there was a good chance it would stay that way for the rest of the period. It was like we crossed a line and got to a better place that no one wanted to leave.

It was long understood among our crew that if any significant rain fell during the day, we were not meeting at the school to play. It seemed like much of the rain that fell anywhere nearby would pool up around the school. Even the basketball courts and the tennis courts would flood. It hardly took much rain at all. For a long time when we were younger, we would all ride to the school when it had rained earlier in the day. We would check things out in the hope that it wasn't too muddy and wet to play ball. It never worked out though, and we had learned over the years how much rain was too much. If it rained enough that day, we were in unspoken agreement that we weren't going to meet up.

We typically paired off on rainy days. The twins would do stuff together if it rained. Scott and Jimmy would hang, or Scott would do things with his older brothers, and Jimmy would tool around in his garage with his sister. Todd and Brian lived just a few houses from each other, so they would meet and do things. Raji never left the house if it rained. He would stay home and play music. Tommy would do things with his brother. Then of course Terry and I were neighbors, so that was an easy one. I never thought much about how rain would separate us until I got older. I wonder why on rainy days it worked out the way it did. Maybe it was just convenient to stay dry and meet with whomever was the closest. But we were never too worried about getting wet. Maybe it was more than that.

Rain limited your fun choices. Atari was always good for having fun on a rainy day. If it wasn't raining too hard, we could ride our bikes to the video store and rent a movie, or there was always the arcade if we could scrounge up some money. If the rain wasn't too hard, we would just ride our bikes around town. That was an example of 'no-money fun'. We were pretty good at no-money fun. This was one of those days. The sun was trying to get through but just couldn't. It drizzled mostly and was dry here and there, so we decided to just ride around.

It took us a long time, and we learned the hard way, but eventually we figured out that we shouldn't wear good clothes out in the rain. This was especially true if we were going to be riding our bikes. Not only would we get soaked, but our back wheels would shoot a line of grime up onto the back of our shirts. Jimmy was smart and handy enough to add a mud guard to his bike. Terry and I had no such smarts or skill, so we just dealt with it. We could have just worn jackets, but that would have made too much sense. Terry had a Kiss concert tee shirt he would wear in the rain. We were smart enough, or maybe it was our Moms that were smart enough, to get us to go with darker colored shirts that we didn't like, so the grime on our backs would blend in as much as possible. That was a concession our moms had to make in light of the fact that we were never going to wear jackets. Terry's Kiss shirt was black. A Kiss concert shirt would have been way too cool to wear in the rain except that his mom had accidentally spilled bleach on it when she was washing clothes. It had big pink spots all over it, so Terry didn't mind getting it dirty. I had a *Mork from Ork* shirt that my grandmother gave me. It was my go-to shirt for a rainy day. It was dark brown, so it helped with the muddy stripe. On the front was a picture of Robin Williams dressed up as Mork with the words 'Nanu Nanu' under him. It was the perfect shirt for getting dirty in the rain.

We decided we would try to ride over to McMahon Park. It had been a while since we were escorted out of the park and all the way out of town, so we were hoping the cops wouldn't recognize us. It seemed less likely that we were going to have any problems since it was just the two of us, rather than the whole crew. The ride still had an added excitement to it since it seemed like we were breaking the rules. It was like a secret mission. I'm sure the cops really couldn't have cared less.

We passed 'my house' as we hit the corner of Thompson and Long. It was still the perfect house for my family, but I didn't like riding past it like I did the first time. I was starting to resent the people who lived there even though I had never so much as set eyes on them. In reality I figured that I was never going to be able to buy that house for my Mom, and we were never gonna live there. I didn't want to look at that house anymore. I was becoming resentful toward the whole town. I turned my head and sped up on my bike to get past it. Terry had to stand up and peddle to catch up to me.

"I didn't know we were having a race."

"Sorry. I just felt like going faster for a second."

When we got to the park there was almost nobody else there. There was a couple of people jogging around on the track, but nobody was playing on any of the fields. The basketball and tennis courts were deserted. The same guy who had kicked us out of the park that day said 'hello' to us as we walked our bikes around. He didn't recognize us as being with the group of the kids he bounced out of the park not too long before that day. We walked around just admiring how perfect everything was. There really wasn't so much as a blade of grass out of place. In the middle of the baseball fields, there was a snack stand. It was closed that day. Terry and I stopped to read the plaques hanging up all over it. It seemed like they won every baseball tournament ever held.

"Look at that."

"1981 Little League World Series Qualifier."

"What does that mean?"

"It means back in '81 they got to play in the Little League World Series."

"There's a Little League World Series?"

"Yeah, there are teams from all over the country and all over the world."

"Serious?"

"How did you know that?"

"I just know."

"So, they made it to the World Series."

"Yeah, but they didn't win it. It just says 'qualifier'. I don't see any others from that year."

"It seems like that's the only thing they didn't win."

"Ohhh, look at that."

On the other side of the snack stand was this huge fenced in compound. I didn't realize what it was when I first saw it. Terry knew instantly. He walked over to where the fencing started and tried to open one of the gates, but it was locked. There was a big sign that had a phone number for coaches to call to reserve time for their teams.

"What is this?"

"It's a batting cage, dummy. Look at this thing. It's huge. There must be a dozen of them. Most towns don't even have one. They got a bunch. You can come here with your whole team and have everyone hitting at once."

"Whoa. How fast do the machines throw?"

"They can throw it as fast as you want. You can set whatever speed you want."

"You kids out without jackets? You're gonna get sick."

"It's not raining that hard."

"Is your coach coming? I didn't think anybody would have batting practice on a day like this."

"We're not on a team. We're just checking it out."

"Oh, ok. You kids wanna hit?"

"It's ok? We can hit?"

Terry was super excited. You could hear it in his voice. I was less enthusiastic at first. I had never had the honor of being struck out by an inanimate object before, and I was not sure I wanted to jump in there. Still, the cages were too nice, and it was just too cool an opportunity to pass up.

"Well, you're supposed to come with your coach, but nobody's here. I can turn on one of the machines and let you hit a few."

"Awesome! Thank you!"

"You guys got bats? We don't keep bats here. The teams bring their bats when they come."

Terry laced his fingers through the fencing hung his head dejectedly. He gave out a hugh sigh. "No, we don't have a bat."

"Just run home and grab a bat. I'll be here until eight. There's lights if it's too dark."

"Ok, we'll be right back."

Lights! We could actually hit under the lights! We were stoked. We hopped back on our bikes and took off for home. Terry owned a bat. We were racing toward Terry's house in fear that the guy who was going to let us hit would change his mind if we took too long getting back. We were pedaling as fast as we could, but Terry's bike still wasn't right. Jimmy got the bike going after something broke that night over the summer, but it was not like it was before that. Terry could only go so fast. I was out in front of him a bit. As we got close to Thompson and Long, a police car turned a corner up ahead and started heading toward us. I was just as happy to turn and not pass *my* house again. We were still operating under the assumption that there was an all-points bulletin out for our arrest. I made a quick turn down the next side street.

"Not this street."

"We have to. The cops."

My adrenaline was rising as we 'evaded' arrest. I was in full fugitive mode. I don't think that bike could have moved any faster than I was making it go that day. The thought of getting back to the park in time to use the batting cage and the exhilaration of running from the police had me at top speed. I wasn't even trying to avoid the puddles. I was loving the way the water would explode into waves on each side of my front tire. I could feel the moisture soaking through the back of my shirt, but I didn't care. I loved it when I got up to a speed where I could hear the wind rushing by. It was then that I realized I was alone. Terry was two blocks back in the middle of the street. I slammed on my brakes.

"TERRY! WHAT ARE YOU DOING? C'MON, WE GOTTA GO!"

He didn't move. He was frozen there in the middle of the street.

"TERRY! TERRY!

I couldn't imagine why he wasn't at full speed trying to get that bat as quickly as we could. He was motionless. His bike must have broke again. It was the only explanation for why he wasn't moving. I started peddling back to him. My legs were starting to feel heavy now. It wasn't like before. I had felt like I could ride like that all day. Now I was feeling every bit of the effort it took to get up to that speed. Backtracking now when it seemed like we needed to be making progress as fast as possible was so frustrating. I was pissed off. When I made it back to Terry, he wasn't trying to fix his bike. He was just straddling it right in the middle of the street. I looked to see if there was anything wrong – I thought maybe the chain popped off, but it seemed fine.

"What are you doing? Is something wrong with your bike? We need to go."

He was staring off to the side at what seemed like nothing. I was making circles around him hoping he would snap out of it and get going.

"Yo, Earth to Terry. Don't you want to hit?"

"That's my house."

I stopped circling and pulled up alongside him.

"What? What are you talking about?"

He was locked in on this house. It was beautiful and huge like all the houses in that town were. There was a big porch that ran the full length of the front of the house. At one end of the porch there was a bench swing and two rocking chairs. On the table between the chairs was a silver jug and two silver glasses. At the other end, the porch extended out into an oval shaped gazebo. The rounded area had a higher roof than the rest of the porch. There was a big round table and benches there. It was big enough that at least ten people to sit there at once. The front walk was a herringbone brick pattern. The same bricks formed two columns at each side of the front stairs. Each pillar had these cool lights on the top. The front door was majestic. It was red and there was a big black knocker in the middle. There were huge glass panes on each side running the full height of the door and a big glass arch above it. Two old timey lights were on at each side of the glass panes. To the left and right of each window on the house hung black shutters. There had to be a dozen windows across the front side of the two stories of the house. There was a huge detached garage on the right side of the house. It had these big barn doors on the front. It looked to be two stories as well. There was a steeple at the top of the garage that matched the one on the top of the main house. The place seemed like a king's palace to us.

"This is where we lived before my dad died."

"What?"

"We used to live here when my dad was alive. We used to play catch over there on the side. He hung a tire swing up on that big tree over there. That was cool. I guess they took it down. He climbed up that tree without a ladder and hung it there. He had an old car that he kept in that garage. We would work on it together. I used to sit there with him sometimes and hand him tools. If it was nice out, we would all go for a ride in it. The top used to come down. He could do anything".

He never looked away from the house as he spoke. It was almost like he was talking to himself.

"There's a pool in the back. There's a cool slide...unless they took that down too."

"Why did you move?"

"We couldn't afford it anymore."

"Terry, what happened to your dad?"

"Let's go. I don't want to go back to the park. Let's get out of here."

"You don't want to hit? But those batting cages were awesome."

"No, let's just go."

I didn't push him on it. I could see that he was as upset now as he was excited back at the park just a few minutes earlier. He was silent as we rode. I was trying to think of something to say but was again coming up with nothing. I had that same feeling as when I was at Jimmy's. I was hating myself for not being able to find the right words. Why is it that twice in a row just a few days apart I couldn't think of anything? I should have learned something from the last time. I was leaving a friend, this time my closest friend, out to dry, and it was the second time in a week that I was doing it. I was so sorry that I ever turned down that street. We should be on our way back to the park now with Terry's bat. He should be as thrilled as he was when he first saw those cages. He should be happy. I was riding alongside him now instead of racing out in front, but he couldn't look at me. It was my fault that all this hurt was raining down on him now.

When we got to our street the light was red, but Terry stood up and ripped right through the intersection. A pick-up truck slammed on his brakes to avoid running him over.

"TERRY!"

I don't think he could hear me over the sound of the pick-up truck's horn. I don't think it would have mattered even if he did hear me. He didn't look back. There was a bunch of cars coming, so I was stuck at the corner for a while. I saw him turn on Second Avenue and he was gone from sight. When the light finally changed, and the traffic let up, I took off as fast as I could go. I got to Second Avenue, but there was no sign of him anywhere. I thought about trying to find him. It was a small town, and there were only so many places to go. If I tried, I was sure that I could find him even though he had a huge head start. His bike wasn't right. I could go much faster than him. I needed to get home though. I was late already. My parents would freak if I didn't show up soon. He left me for a reason anyway. He didn't want to be around me. If I found him, what was I going to say? I still didn't know. I was spinning around in circles in my head and on my bike. I looked down Second Avenue and then back toward our street, then again down Second Avenue and again toward home. I finally took off toward my house. The rain was picking up. It was steady now. I was getting what I asked for. It was raining hard, but now I didn't want it to be.

I rocketed the few blocks back to my house. I skidded in the water outside my garage and slammed into the garage door. I ran inside and out of the rain.

"What was that?"

"Nothing"

"It didn't sound like 'nothing'? Did you crash into the garage? It sounded like something crashed into the garage door."

"Nothing crashed. Leave me alone."

"Hey! You don't talk like that to your mother. You're late, and she's asking you a question."

I just went in my room and closed the door. My Dad came in right after me.

"Hey, you don't just ignore us when we're talking to you. That's disrespectful. What's going on with you."

"Nothing. I'm fine."

"Nothing my ass. Why are you acting like this?"

My mom came into my room too. I didn't say anything. I just wanted them to leave, so I could be alone. I started taking off my wet clothes and changing into some dry ones.

"Start talking, Richard!"

She never used my full name unless she was really mad. I wasn't going to get them out of my room without an explanation.

"Terry left me. OK. He rode away from me down Second Street, and I don't know where he went."

"Well, did you guys have a fight? Why did he do that?"

"No, he's upset because we rode down his old street and saw the house he used to live in before his dad died. It's my fault because I turned down that street and he didn't want to go that way."

"I'll go next door and talk to John."

"Why do you have to tell him? It's probably fine. He'll just go home when he's ready."

My Dad left the room to go next door.

"It's not fine. Don't you hear that? It's pouring outside and it's dark. He could hit by a car. It's hard to see a kid on his bike at night when it's raining. He could fall of his bike and get hurt. We need to find him."

That all sounded like crazy talk to me. He wasn't going to get hit by a car. Why would he fall off his bike? We never fell off our bikes. It all just seemed like stupid stuff parents would say. The first bolt of thunder was so loud that it sounded like it was in our attic. It shook us. I could see my Mom flinch at the sound.

"You see. It's getting worse outside. He shouldn't be out in this."

She came and sat next to me on my bed.

"This isn't your fault. He misses his dad. You would miss yours too. But you can't just ignore us when we are talking to you. You have to answer us when we ask you something."

"It's my fault. I turned down that street. He didn't want to go there. We could be hitting at the batting cages now. I knew he was sad, and I couldn't say anything. The same thing happened with Jimmy. I never know what to do. Nobody can help anybody."

"Wait, what's this about Jimmy now?"

My Dad walked back into my room.

"John's going to drive around and try to find him. Should we call Mary at the hospital?"

"No, don't call her. I don't want him to get in trouble."

"He's not in trouble, Richie. We're just worried about him."

"She gave me a number for her at work. Look in my address book by the phone."

"Oh, this is great."

My Dad walked out of my room and started paging through my Mom's address book.

"Dad, stop. You don't have to tell his mom."

I was trying to take the address book from him. He was fending me off with one hand and trying to look up the number with the other.

"Stop it. C'mon. What if something happens and we don't call her? She would be mad that we didn't let her know."

"Nothing is going to happen."

"Hey, calm down. I told you he's not in trouble. We just need to get him home."

It was like a family wrestling match at the phone. My Mom was pulling me away from my Dad who was trying to find the number while he was fending me off. I was grabbing at the address book. The thunder was getting even louder, and lightning flashed so often it seemed like it there was a war outside between day and night. The light came in through the kitchen window every second or so, on then off and on again. I was losing the wrestling match. My Dad started dialing. Then someone knocked at the front door.

"That must be John. Maybe he found him."

My Dad hung up the phone. I exhaled. My mom opened the door. Terry looked like he jumped into a pool with all his clothes on.

"Terry! You're soaked."

He was shivering a little and his eyes were bloodshot. My Dad ran into the bathroom and came out with a towel. He started drying him off as my Mom wrapped her arms around him and walked him to the couch.

'Richie, get Terry one of your shirts."

I ran into my room and came back with a tee shirt. I handed it to Terry. He used it to wipe the water from his eyes.

"I'm sorry."

"Why?"

"Hey, we were worried about you. Are you okay?"

"Can I please stay over tonight?"

"I think you should be home tonight, Terry. You're Uncle is out looking for you. We were just about to call your Mom."

"No. No. No. No. Please. Please. Please. Please. I can't. I can't. I can't."

He was shaking and was having trouble breathing. He reached out and was holding my Mom's shoulders.

"Please. Please. I can't go home. I can't be with him. Please."

"What's wrong, Terry. You can't be with who?"

"Him. Him. I can't be with him. I can't be with him. I CAN'T BE WITH HIM!"

My Mom and Dad gave each other a look. I saw them and they looked at me as if they wished they could send me to my room. They moved on each side of Terry. My Mom was holding his hand in hers, and my Dad was rubbing his back. I stood across from them.

"Are you talking about your uncle, Terry? Why can't you be with him?"

The question was obviously for Terry but my Mom was looking at me as she finished it. I could tell she knew the answer, and she didn't really want me to hear it. I don't think she or my dad wanted to hear the answer either. It was like one of those things you would say where you immediately wished you could reach out and grab the words out of the air and pull them back into your mouth. I knew he was talking about Uncle John, but I didn't know why. I think my parents knew why already. I think they knew why, and they knew that as much as they didn't want him to say it out loud, that they had to let Terry speak. I was finding it hard not to cry. I didn't know why I was sad. I was just upset at seeing my friend so upset.

When Terry first started it was hard for him to talk. He was having a hard time breathing he was crying so hard. My Mom was holding him tight. My Dad went into the kitchen and came back with a glass of water. He handed it to Terry and walked over to the front window. Terry was saying some things that I really didn't understand. My Mom was crying now too and giving me those looks adults would give kids when they didn't want you to hear or know what was going on. My Dad had his back to us, but I could see him wiping away tears.

"Boy, it's really coming down now."

None of us were interested in the weather. I don't think my Dad was interested in telling us about it either. He was just trying to hide his face for a minute. Terry took some of the water and calmed down enough to speak more easily. He told us what had been going on at his house on the nights when his Mom was at work and his Uncle would stay with him. I was as confused by it all as I was upset. My understanding of sex at the time was limited to a couple of R-rated movies and a Playboy magazine Scott found in his basement and showed us one time when his parents weren't home. None of this made any sense to me. They were both boys. Terry liked girls. They were related. In our minds Uncle John was an old person. I was having trouble processing any of it. I didn't understand why Terry didn't say anything the first time it happened. I didn't understand why he didn't tell his mom. Why didn't he tell me? Todd never said anything about his dad hitting him. The Simpson's never spoke of their mom's drinking. I thought about how Jimmy didn't tell anyone about his dad beating his mom. Why didn't they just say something. It would have made things better.

My Dad walked back from the window and stood next to me facing away from my Mom and Terry toward the back of the house. He put his hand on my shoulder and was giving it a squeeze every so often. I looked up at him and he mouthed 'I love you' to me. Terry kept going and things kept sounding worse and worse. My Mom was holding him and looking to me every so often. She was sorry for what he was going through. She was sorry I was hearing any of it. She was sorry I had to learn about these things this way. Every so often she would tell Terry 'it's going to be okay now', but I didn't believe it. I didn't think anything would be okay for him ever again.

At some point my mind stopped trying process the things Terry was saying. I started thinking about how all this went on right next door to us, and none of us had any idea. I could almost touch Terry's house from my bedroom, and I didn't truly know what his life was like. He was right next door, and I didn't know how much pain he was in. He was my best friend, and I knew so little about him. I didn't know that he lived in the next town before he moved next door. I didn't know how his dad died. I didn't know what his uncle was doing to him. How could I live so close to someone and not know? I started thinking about how Terry would flinch away when his uncle would mess up his hair. I had always thought that it was just a friendly way to say hello. He did the same to me. But it wasn't just when he would mess up our hair. Terry would flinch away every time his uncle reached out to touch him. I could see it now. I could play it all out in my mind now - all the times I was with Terry and his uncle and the way Terry tried to avoid any contact with him. Now it made sense, but now it was too late.

It was like Terry's words were eating away the fog that I had lived in up until that point. But it wasn't just Terry. I lived less than a mile from all of my friends and knew so little about any of them. I thought about Todd. How did I manage to miss what Todd was dealing with? I saw the way his dad was basically carrying him by his neck out of the school that day. I could see the bruises on his back when his shirt came up after Marie ran him over at the plate. They weren't from baseball. It wasn't just on days that he did anything wrong either. I remember him limping around sometimes for no reason when we were playing at the school. I can remember him flinching when I would give him a pat on the back after a good play. Why was it clear now, and I had no idea before?

How about Mrs. Simpson? She wasn't just a bad driver. It was seven o'clock in the morning when she would take Billy and Marie to the bus stop, and she was already drinking. Nobody drives that bad. Why did I not realize? Why was I so stupid? The twins could never get out of that car fast enough in the morning. Mrs. Simpson always had a drink with her. I could see it now but before that night I never noticed a thing.

What about Jimmy? I lived just a few blocks from Jimmy, and I had no idea that his dad would beat up his mom. I could throw a rock from my house to his, and I still had no idea what was going on in his life. I started thinking about his little sister shaking when she heard her parents arguing. Terry was shaking like that now. I wanted to throw some headphones over his head and drown out the pain he was in. I wanted to sit him a chair in the garage and play music in his ears that would let him forget it all. I wished there was a song that could do that. Now I remembered it all. Now I saw it all. I only put it together now as Terry was tearing away the veil I had over my eyes. I could see his lips were moving, but I couldn't hear him anymore. It was like he was silently chewing away the darkness that I was living in.

My Mom and Dad wanted it to stay dark for me a while longer. They wanted the chance to decide when I would see the light. They were sad not only for Terry but for me. I could tell it in their faces. They were hoping for more time before I had to know about these things. I was so lucky I thought. My parents were great. I hadn't realized until I could see how horrible my friends had it. My parents gave me a great life. I had always thought of them before as an inconvenience that I needed to deal with. They would embarrass me when I was trying to be cool. They had it so much harder than I had imagined. There was all this chaos around us, literally all around us, and they managed to shield me from it for so long. I could have had it so much worse. I don't know how they dealt with it all. Up until that moment I felt like we lived in the center of the world. It was just the center of New Jersey. It was a small town, and it seemed like everybody knew everybody, but it wasn't really that way either. Nobody really knew anybody. Nobody could help anybody.

The knock at the door broke the silence.

"NOOO!! PLEASE!!"

Terry exploded from the couch and darted toward the back of my house. My Mom caught up to him and held on.

"It's okay. It's okay. It's okay. I'm not gonna let you go. You're safe now. It's okay."

My Dad went to the door after he made sure that my Mom and Terry had some distance between them and the monster outside my house. I stood behind my Dad as he opened the door. He gave me a look to see if I was ready. I shook my head to tell him it as okay.

"Oh, there you are. Thank God!"

Uncle John stepped into the doorway, and my Dad reached out and blocked his way. Uncle John looked at him and my Dad was shaking his head.

"No."

"No. What?"

Uncle John gave my Dad a confused look. He looked around my Dad to where Terry was standing with my Mom draped around him.

"What's going on, Terry? What's wrong?"

He made another attempt at entering the house, but again my Dad stiff armed him at the doorway. Rain was coming in through the front door. I could see Uncle John getting wet with the rain. Some of the water made its way down from the top of his head into his eyes. That was annoying him as much as my dad keeping him there in the rain was. He wiped the water away angrily.

"Tim, C'mon."

"No."

The Thunder was making me flinch. It made us all flinch. It was deafening. The sound was even louder now that the front door was open. The lightning flashed around the dark spaces where Uncle John stood in the doorway. I could see him getting smaller and the light getting larger. He was shrinking right there in front of us. His face changed. He could tell now that Terry wasn't just upset about seeing his old house or missing his Dad.

"Terry. C'mon, Buddy. Let's go home now. Let's stop bothering these nice people. We gave them enough trouble tonight."

He wasn't looking at Terry anymore. He was speaking down into the ground. He knew Terry wasn't going anywhere and he wasn't getting inside. I wasn't going to let him anywhere near my friend. He started shaking as he spoke, and now he was slowly folding up like there was a slow unrelenting pressure above his head grinding him down into the ground.

"Terry. Terry. What ya been telling these people, Terry? What ya been telling these people, Terry? You making up stories, Terry?"

I turned to look behind me. Terry turned away from the front door and buried his face in my Mom's shoulder. Uncle John was falling to the ground in slow motion. He was the one shaking and crying now. It was like there was a hammer over his head swinging down on him driving him into the floor. I wanted to hold that hammer. I wanted to pound him over the head with it and sink him into the ground. He reached around his stomach with both arms like there was a sting in his gut that was unbearable. He was slowly falling to the ground.

"I'm sorry. I'm so sorry, Terry. I'm so sorry. I'm so...."

He was making noises like he was going to be sick. His breaths were audible and strange. He crumbled down to his knees in the doorway, his arms around his stomach. He was crooked up against one side of the doorway. He never looked up from the floor again. The rain was soaking him now. He was drenched. He was like a heaving pile of wet garbage in my doorway now. I thought that it must be awful to be him. It must be the worst thing in the world to be him at that moment. I never wanted to do something so awful that it would make me crumble down to my knees like he did. I never wanted people to look at me the way we were all looking at him. I never wanted to feel that sting in my gut. I could almost feel it looking at the way he was holding himself.

My Dad looked back at me and gave me a nod. It was like we had won a victory. I saw that look before. He would look at me like that when I was younger and woke up in the middle of the night afraid that there was a monster in my room. He would turn on the light and walk with me as we searched out the intruder. He would hold my hand as we looked under the bed and in my closet. We slayed so many monsters together. We kept a monster from getting into our house that night. Maybe Terry was wrong that nobody could help anybody. Maybe we were at least able to help him some that night. We could help him from now on. I took a look back to see how he was doing. It looked like my mom was holding him up now. He seemed exhausted. I wished that I could have saved him from all the things his uncle had done to him all those years. I wished that I could have gone back in time and stopped it. We did help keep his uncle away that night. It was a small win. It was something.

I started thinking about the rest of my friends and what I didn't know about them. Was there something awful going on in their lives that I didn't know? Was there some way I could help them? I started thinking about Kelly. I was thinking about how her dad locked her away in that house. That must be so awful for her. Why would he keep her there like a prisoner? It was always so dark in there. How could she stay in the dark like that. I wanted to bring her out into the light. She didn't do anything wrong. Why wasn't she allowed out to play with us? What kind of life was that – being stuck in the house day after day? That was no kinda life for a kid, to be caged like that. What if her dad was beating her? What if that's why he didn't let her out – because people would see the bruises? Maybe that's why she was stuck in there every day? That was why he put the sneaker on my bike that day. To warn me that he could get to me if he wanted to. He was warning me not to tell his secret. I was trying to think to that night in the hedges at the Mercer's. Did I miss anything? Were there any bruises that I didn't notice. It was dark, but that lightning bug was shining on her. I closed my eyes and tried to remember. I could see her face and how pretty she was but were there any marks? I tried to remember what she looked like in the light.

Maybe he wasn't beating her. Maybe he was doing the same things as Uncle John was doing to Terry. Maybe he was making her do those same things. There were no marks on Terry. There was nothing for us to see. There was no way to look at him and know what was happening. There were no marks on Kelly. That must be it. He's keeping her in that house so he could keep her from telling anyone. He was doing the same thing just down the street. I had to do something. I had to help her.

"There's no marks on her."

"What?"

"I have to help her."

"What? Who?"

I leapt over what was left of Uncle John in our doorway and into my front yard. I was soaked almost instantly as my feet hit the ground. It was hard to open my eyes all the way as the rain sheeted down. The water poured down my face into my eyes. It was cool and it tasted fresh on my lips. The thunder clapped so loud that it rattled my insides. I could hear the sizzle of the lightning each time it flashed. I saw my whole neighborhood as it struck, then the houses disappeared again for a moment until the next, on then off and on again. My feet were cold in the street. The water rushed like a river toward the school. I felt the sweat on my body and the grime on my back from riding around that day rinse down my legs and into the street. As I sprinted clean and wet toward Kelly's house, the lightning bathed our neighborhood over and over again in white light. It looked like quick glimpses of an old movie. I looked up at the house, again it seemed dark and uninhabited. The red and blue replaced the white of the lightning. The colors were racing across the front of Kelly's house. I turned as the cars pulled right up in the front yard. Four police cars stopped right on the curb, and a plain black car almost ran me over. Eight cops in rain gear sprinted for the front door. A woman got out of the plain car in front of me. Her jacket said 'Child Protection Services'. She stood near the car with an umbrella and a clipboard.

"What are you doing out here in this?"

I was too afraid to speak.

"You should go home. Go home, son."

I just took a few steps back. I wanted to see Kelly. I wanted to see what was happening. The storm started easing up. I could see the flashlights spinning around in the house. I could still hear the thunder lightly in the distance, over someone else's town. The rain was light now. After a few minutes, one of the cops came to the doorway and signaled for the lady to come inside. After she disappeared inside, the cop came out to the top step.

"You people need to move back."

People? What people?

I wasn't alone anymore. Some of the neighbors were standing in the street just behind me. My Dad walked up next to me and held an umbrella over us. I turned to look back to our house. He should have been standing guard for Terry.

"They're fine. He's gone."

"We have to tell the police."

"We will. He won't get away."

After a while, the lady from the black car emerged from the house with a small suitcase. She was holding Kelly's hand. She walked Kelly out to the plain car.

"Goodbye, Richie."

I didn't want to say goodbye. I didn't want this to be the last that I ever saw of her, but I knew that it would be. The lady unlocked the car and loaded Kelly into the back seat. Through the droplets on the window, I could see that she was crying now. I wished that I could make her stop. I didn't want her to be sad. For a minute I thought that this might be the worst way for things to turn out. They were going to take her away, and I would never see her again. If she stayed in that house, at least there was a chance that I might see her from time to time. I knew she couldn't stay in that house though. I knew she couldn't live that way, like a prisoner. I wanted to make her stop crying. I wanted her to look like she did that time in the hedges in the Mercer's backyard. I wanted her face to light up like that again. She was so happy that night. I knew she would never light up like that if she stayed in that house. I knew she needed to get out.

The woman got into the front of the car. She backed up off the curb and sped away. I watched the car drive down my street until it was too dark to see it anymore. Two of the policemen came out of the house with Kelly's dad. He was handcuffed. They led him to the back of one of their cars. The red and blue lights were racing across his face. He looked to all of us standing there in the street in front of his house.

"I love my daughter. I would do anything for her. Anything. I had to. I had to get her out of there."

He wasn't scary anymore. His voice was breaking as he spoke. He wasn't looking at us as he finished speaking. He was looking down at the ground. I felt sorry for him. One of the cops put his hand on the top of Kelly's father's head and started pushing it down. He fell into the back seat of the car. One of the policemen started the car and sped away. I looked back at the house. I hated that house. I hated it so much that I wished that I could tear it down. I didn't want anyone else imprisoned there. I wished it would have fallen down after they got Kelly out of there. I wanted all the pain she must have felt in there to blow out all of the walls so that the roof would crumble to the ground.

"Let's go home, Champ."

"What's gonna happen to her?"

"I don't know, Richie. I just hope things are better for her now."

Terry's Mom's car was in front of our house now. She would need to know the whole story. Terry was probably in there right now explaining everything the same way he had told us just a little while ago. It must be terrible for him to have to tell the story over and over. He was going to have to tell the Police too. I felt like it was all too much. I couldn't hear it again. I couldn't watch Terry say it over again for his Mom. I should be strong for him, but it was too much for one night. As we made our way across the street, my Dad could sense how I was dreading the scene in our living room.

"Dad, I..."

"It's okay. When we get in there, just go in your room and close the door. It's fine. Me and your Mom can deal with this."

I felt a huge sense of relief. My parents would shield one more time. As we walked in the house, Terry's Mom was holding him in the front room. Terry had his head buried in his Mom's chest. She was crying and telling him that it wasn't his fault. I was glad he had his eyes hidden away. I didn't want to make eye contact with him as I walked away toward my room. I didn't want him to see me leaving him. I needed to escape everything that happened that night. I didn't want to hear any more crying. I didn't want to see any more pain. I started feeling ashamed that I wasn't strong enough to stay in the living room. I got to the door of my room and the feeling of failure was coming over me again. I was in the hallway at school again watching Todd's dad carry him past me by the neck. I could see Mr. Hughes feeling helpless in middle of the hallway. I was at the bus stop again watching Mrs. Simpson slam her car into the Towney's garbage can. I could see Marie and Billy afraid and ashamed and scrambling as quickly as possible out of the back seat. I was in Jimmy's garage again. I saw his sister quaking in her chair. I was seeing Jimmy trying to look away from me as his eyes filled with tears and he worked on his bike. I was in the middle of the street again with Terry. I was watching him as all those memories of his Dad rushed into his eyes. I was riding next to him in silence again as he struggled with that overwhelming loss and the pain of what was happening to him each night. I was in the driveway again as they took Kelly out of that house and out of my life forever. I could hear her saying goodbye again and I was silent as my last chance to say something to her slipped away. Enough. Enough. Not again. Not ever again.

I turned and walked over to where Terry was standing with his Mom. I wrapped my arms around him and squeezed tight.

"Richie."

"I'm here. I'm right here."

As I finished up the dishes, I could see them. They were bright against the night. They danced around the tree in our backyard. They were as brilliant as they were all those years before. Ever since that summer I tried to make a point to never miss a chance to stop and to watch them again. My wife captured one in her hands and knelt next to my daughter. I had seen that look on her face on another young girl years ago. All the wonder and how perfect my little girl looked brought me back in time. My wife placed one in the center of my daughter's hand. It stayed there for so long – safe and secure, brightening the summer night. They never seemed to stay so long in my hands. My little girl's face was just perfect. The light in her eyes was a beauty beyond anything I had ever seen. While I was seeing it with my eyes, I was feeling it in my chest. After a moment it lifted off back toward the others.

"Again, Mommy. Again!"

My wife laughed and gave me a nod at the kitchen window. She softly placed another one in my daughter's hand. She was over the moon. She ran over to the window where I was watching.

"Daddy, did you see?"

"I saw."

She turned and ran into the kitchen.

"Daddy, did you see it? Did you see me holding it? It was lighting up."

"I know. I saw it all. That was so awesome!"

"I want to get a jar. I want to get one to stay in my room with me and light up my room all night."

She was rummaging through some of the kitchen cabinets as she spoke. I picked her up and gave her a big hug.

"Oh, are you sure you want to do that?"

"Yeah, I'm sure. It can be all mine. It's going to be great to have one live in my room all the time."

I sat her down on the counter and gave her a kiss.

"Can we talk for a minute about the lightning bugs, Baby?"

"Sure Daddy. Do want one to have one in your room? I can get you one for your room."

"They're pretty when the light up, aren't they?"

"Yeah, really pretty."

"Do you know why they light up like they do?"

--The End--